AF447982

SPLIT DECISION
DAVID PERLMUTTER

SPLIT DECISION

I.

Jody Ryder wiped the beads of perspiration that had gathered on top of her pelt, sighed, and tried to prepare herself for the next round of the latest athletic contest she had become embroiled in. As the star athlete of Hudson High School- and a heroic, super-powered, teenage canine robot to boot- such things were not uncommon to her. Most often, she was able to walk away from them, bloodied but unbowed, due to her remarkable power, manifested in her swift and agile physique and intelligent yet artificial positronic brain. Today would be no exception.

What *was an* exception was that she was *not* playing one of the sports where her combination of speed, agility and strength would have been of greatest assistance to her- football, rugby, field and ice hockey or gymnastics (all of which she lettered in, by the way), but a slightly more genteel sport also requiring these abilities for success. Tennis.

Her opponent, a green skinned alien being resembling a humanized pterodactyl (as much as Jody and the majority of the audience resembled- and were- humanized dogs), had tested Jody to her limits that day. Each of them had won one set, and the games had been fierce enough to tear the covers off most of the balls on the court- necessitating a rain-delay type halt in the middle of the match to fetch another full case. Jody, who in her robot hero guise could lift thousands of pounds of Earth's green land with her paws, was the main cause of this, although her opponent was certainly no pushover in the power department. She, as an exchange student at Hudson's great rival for athletic supremacy in the city of Hugopolis- Clinton- had torn up the courts as much as Jody had, and had made their inevitable clash in the finals here and now something to be anticipated. Despite this, but very much in synch with the genteel behavior of the sport, there had been no McEnroe-style trash talking or temper tantrums aimed at the ref. Jody, in particular, was too good a sport to resort to such things. If the athletes felt any sense of intimidation or rivalry with each other, it was something they had deliberately chosen to keep to themselves.

It had been, as already noted above, a vicious and tightly fought match nonetheless, but the tooth and claw fight was coming to an end. In this final set, Jody had taken control early, and blazed her way across it. Now, she needed only one more game to secure victory, and a paralyzing hush had come across the velodrome where the game was being played, as everyone was anticipating Jody's next move. She had, after all, control of the ball, and the game could not proceed until she chose to act.

Jody acted.

Having wiped the artificially produced sweat off her orange and white pelt, adjusted her red headband beneath her large, overly canine ears, and smoothed out the dress whites she was wearing, she raised her racquet with the ball against it upright.

"Service!" she said softly, so her opponent would be aware that the game was commencing again, and promptly fired the ball powerfully at her.

For the next few minutes, they knocked the ball around with athletic grace, lob backed by smash, smash backed by lob, until Jody's opponent grazed the net and caused the ball to bounce back onto her side of the court. The audience applauded politely, and Jody, knowing victory was now in sight, let down her guard slightly.

That was a mistake.

Her opponent, seemingly sensing the change in approach, blasted the ball back at Jody three successive times, causing her to win the game. Jody looked at the scoreboard- and loudly gasped. Her opponent was only one game away from tying her- and another from taking the set and defeating her!

Knowing this, Jody tightened up. In the last possible game of the set, when the ball came back at her, she struck back. With a powerful stroke of musculature reminiscent much more of DiMaggio or Mantle than King or Navratilova, she struck the ball so hard that it flew out of the velodrome and directly into Earth's orbit, leaving both her opponent and the audience stunned and Jody mortifyingly embarrassed. Even *she* could be embarrassed about how strong she was, especially since she, unlike them, was fully aware of how enhanced abilities were as much a deficit as an asset in gaining and keeping friends.

This profound silence did not last long, for the crowd cheered loudly when her victory had been established. Even her opponent, when they met for the traditional shaking of....appendages, was impressed.

"You do know we're supposed to be playing *tennis,* right?" she said humorously.

"Yeah," Jody admitted. "But I play so *many* sports I don't know the difference between them sometimes."

That got a laugh that continued as her opponent exited the court, even though Jody was speaking seriously. That confused her. But, even more confusing was the fact that, within that seemingly endless band of good feeling towards her in the stands, she had a strange feeling that there was a new, non-athletic opponent was out there, wanting to attack and kill her for something that she knew nothing about but was somehow responsible for causing....

II.

"No fair! You SUCK! BOO!"

The owner of the voice uttering those words was a spectator in the crowd of the match, but she was hardly as impressed as the others at Jody's performance. Rather, she was finding it hard to conceal her hatred for the robot. Which was odd, for she, as a professional "hero" herself, shared Jody's avocation.

Jefferson Ball, to give this individual her right name, was as notorious and infamous as Jody was praised and esteemed. For one thing, their characters, in spite of their joint "profession", were diametrically at odds. While Jody committed herself to physical and moral excellence befitting her inflated stature (which, as a robot, it was relatively easy for her to achieve and gain), Jefferson was just the opposite. Although descended from a long line of genetically endowed "freaks"- and with the enormous strength and speed (rivalling and something surpassing Jody's) to prove it- Jefferson did not conform to traditional American or Christian (whatever *that* was) beliefs regarding heroism. As a heroic robot, Jody used her abilities to help others without desire for recompense. Jefferson, in contrast, usually did not get involved in such things unless there was something in it for her, preferably money (which she was bad with), liquor or boys (both of which she was very much addicted to.) But both, when roused, were fierce forces of righteousness, defeating any forces of evil or anything else which stood in their way easily. However, in spite of living in the exact same town at the exact same time, they had never yet crossed paths, even when they faced similar enemies.

They certainly had heard of each other, however. Jefferson, in particular, was aware of the new supposed "threat" posed to her by the "young turk" in robotic form she was now railing against. Particularly onerous to her was the fact that Jody, in her scholastic incarnation, had broken every single record Jefferson had herself set when she had been a Hudson student not so long ago. Records, it should be said, that Jefferson and her peers had both assumed would live forever. Jefferson had not taken it well, as she did not generally do when the odds were against her.

Consequently, she was now bellowing threats at the robot, under the influence of a now half-empty bottle of peach Schnapps she had just begun draining, and in spite of the fact that Jody was now leaving the court and likely couldn't hear her, anyway.

"Come up here and FIGHT me, you metal faced glory stealer!" Jefferson barked, standing bolt upright in the monogrammed black bikini and boots which was her trademark- and often, only- look. "I'll rip your *head* off and piss in your *thorax!*"

Jefferson would likely have uttered more threats, and more profane ones at that, were it not for the fact that she then vomited, loudly and violently, over those sitting in front of her. Outraged, said beings called for security, and Jefferson was ejected out onto the street, in spite of the protestations she made about how "celebrities" like her should not be *treated* like this.

Upon landing, she came face to face with her one and only friend, Major Hamilton Pomeranian (Star Soldiers- Ret.), who looked up at her with the strange mix of admiration and hatred that normally constituted their relationship. Hamilton, who wore her black dashiki, white T shirt, camouflage pants and black boots as often as Jefferson did her bikini, had left the velodrome without a word as soon as Jefferson uncorked her smuggled in Schnapps bottle, perfectly aware of where, how and why things were going to be going as they were.

"What the hell is *wrong* with you?" Hamilton snapped at her friend. "This is a *tennis* match, not a HOCKEY game!"

"All sports are the same," Jefferson mumbled, in a lame attempt at defense.

"No, they're NOT!" answered Hamilton. "You *might* be able to get away with acting like a *lout* when you're watching a *team* sport, but *tennis* is *different*. The crowd actually shows some *respect* for the athletes, for one thing."

"Did *you* letter in six sports when *you* were in high school, *shorty*?" Jefferson said, needling Hamilton on account of her small frame, which, nevertheless, was very powerful at times.

"No," Hamilton began reluctantly. "Just one. But I...."

"Then *don't* tell me I don't know *anything* about *sports*!"

Jefferson punctuated this statement by using her now empty Schnapps bottle to throw a Hail Mary pass across the parking lot, where it shattered, feet away, into a thousand pieces.

"This is about *Jody Ryder, isn't* it?" Hamilton said, reading her friend like a book.

"DON'T MENTION HER NAME TO ME!" Jefferson roared.

"Just because she broke all of your precious "records"...."

"My *legacy*!"

"...does *not* call for you to declare a *vendetta* on her!"

"Oh, *yes it does*!"

"It does *not*! You *forget* that Jody Ryder is a *hero*, even more so than *you* at times!"

"You miserable...I thought you were my *friend*!"

"Even *friends* have to tell each other the *truth* sometimes, Jefferson! She's *also* just as powerful as *you* are. And a lot more *humane*..."

"*HUMANE*? *She's* a ROBOT!"

"She *saves* people from peril without thinking of herself- something *you* are only *rarely* capable of doing!"

"I assume," Jefferson said, "that you're *not* going to help me *kill* her then..."

"No!" said a firm but clearly appalled Hamilton as she turned heel on her friend. "More than likely, *you'd* be the one killed. And, honestly, that'd be an *improvement* over how you're acting right now!"

"Fine!" Jefferson snarled as Hamilton walked off. "I can take care of her *myself, TRAITOR*!"

And she stalked on home to prepare to do just that.

III.

There was a flourish of activity on the tennis court grounds- including the presentation to Jody of a trophy nearly as big as she was, which she faked groaning under to look "good" and preserve her secret robotic identity- before Jody had a chance to change via her programming into street clothes and confide her fears to somebody.

Like Jefferson Ball, she had only one "somebody" to do this to, and his words mattered more to her than anything else in the world.

Samuel J. Poodle, familiarly known as "Sam", was Jody's classmate at Hudson, and they had become firm friends ever since Jody had publicly defended him from bullying. This bullying had come about because Sam was homosexual, as divisive a thing to be in this future time as it had been in the past. Jody, however, felt it made him more accepting and understanding than the other boys, especially regarding her own "status", and accepted him as a friend purely for that reason alone.

Sam also, however, had a more serious job in Jody's life than merely being her companion. As she was the creation of the Robotics department of American Intelligence, Jody's activities were required to be examined on a regular basis so that she could not use her robotic abilities to betray her masters. That exact situation had happened with two of her prototypes, and, from the evidence, needed to be avoided at all costs. Thus, Jody, after meeting Sam, had volunteered him as her monitor, who would report her activities faithfully to the higher ups when requested, power her up when the electronic circuitry supplying her super-canine abilities began to wane, and discipline her when she had actually or conceivably breached protocol by using the exact same circuitry by which she was powered against her. Sam did not especially like this latter aspect of the job at all, as he was an especially sensitive boy, particularly to the suffering of friends like Jody, but he still did not hesitate to discipline Jody if she got on his nerves. Which was more often than you might think.

He was, naturally, waiting for her when she emerged from the lockers, now, her true strength asserting itself as she handled her heavy trophy just like the lighter tennis racquet she had handled earlier. However, she expressed none of the gleeful joy of the champion, but a surprisingly downcast expression, as if, somehow, she sensed she was being watched by invisible eyes. He saw this in her immediately. Just as she noticed that he was (again!), despite her best discouragement, wearing the maroon-colored skirt he usually favored rather than pants, along with a sweater of the same color, with a large "H" prominently displayed on both parts. For, when he and Jody were not engaged in derring-do as secret agents, Sam was cheering on in her athletic endeavors as the formidable head of Hudson's cheerleading squad.

"Are you *down* again, J.R.?" Sam asked. "After what you *did* today?"

"Dial it down, Sam," Jody answered, handing him her trophy. The weight of it buckled his knees and he fell to the ground, reflecting the fact that he did not possess anywhere near her physical muscle power. However, he spryly got to his feet again once she took it back.

"I'm *not* down," Jody continued. "Far from it, actually. But I *am* feeling suspicious about something."

"What?" Sam asked, with the genuine concern she appreciated, although he also crossed his arms and lowered his eyebrows suspiciously as he said this.

"All through the match," Jody said, "I could swear I heard someone *cursing* me. And *goading* me to come up and *fight* her!"

"Which you obviously didn't do," said Sam, "owing to the fact that you haven't a scratch on you."

"Please, Sam!" Jody said coyly, batting her eyelids in a flirtatious way, knowing full well Sam wouldn't potentially harm her for doing this. "I was otherwise engaged! Besides, I couldn't possibly find that one person right out in the open, in such a big crowd. It wasn't like she was sitting in the front row...."

"She?" Sam asked.

"Oh, don't be so surprised, Sam! I have *girl* rivals. Just like I have *boy* enemies..."

"But not too many away from the fields of glory, J.R. And, when you go on red diaper patrol,"- here Sam referred to Jody's superhero suit, a monogrammed one-piece red swimsuit-like garment- "you gotta admit that it's pretty much a sausage fest..."

"What about Gabagool, the witch queen of Pluto? We had to *dethrone* her, remember?"

"Okay, *her*. But she was an *old crone*. And you and she didn't exactly scrap in the ring, if I remember correctly," Sam said as he threw a mock "punch" at her. "You shot your lasers at her, and she threw spells at you and me, and then you lifted up her castle and dropped it down on top of her to kill her off...."

"Okay, okay! Stop *reminding* me about me being a *female Hercules*, will ya? I embarrassed myself enough today *as it is* with that *last shot*. And, *if* you're implying that I *couldn't* square off in the ring with a *girl*..."

"Not at all! I only mentioned it because you yourself said that the mysterious voice taunting you on the court was *female* in nature."

"Hang on, Sam! I couldn't hear her very well 'cause of the crowd- if it *was* a "her". It easily could have been a member of *your* tribe, for all I know..."

"There *are* some of us who are like that," Sam mused. "Only they usually have *butcher* voices than mine!" He held his paws together and mooned like a teenage girl thinking of a crush- until Jody flicked him on the nose.

"Stop it!" Jody said. "I'm *serious* about this, Sam. I don't *want* some crazy girl coming after me. God knows, I have enough trouble fending off the *boys*, without having someone with the same *equipment* as me wanting a piece of me, too!"

"It might not be a sex thing, Jody," Sam reminded her, assuming a playful "fighting" stance as he did. "She might just be a villainess trying to make trouble for you by taunting you. Calling out publicly for you to wrestle her might just be a way of luring you into a trap."

"Well, villainess or not," Jody said, "I'll wait until *she* decides to make a move, *whatever* it may be. And, if it turns out that she *is* bad news for me, sexual or otherwise, I'll still be able to drop her like a ton of bricks. You know me, Sam. I'm too busy with my sports and super stuff to even *think* about being out of shape!"

"Well, *I'd* always be in shape, too, if *I* was a robot!"

"Are you *implying* something, *Sam?*" an offended Jody blazed.

"No- God, no, Jody!" Sam nervously said as he pulled the collar of his sweater. "I'm just saying that you're not *mortal* like the rest of us, and so...."

She picked him up and threw him onto the nearest bench, smashing it into firewood as she did.

"STOP REMINDING ME THAT I'M A *FREAK!*" she screamed. "I get enough of that kind of crap from *everyone else*. I don't need it from *YOU!*"

She ran outside, crying, with her trophy in hand. Sam, once he recovered, ran out after her and found her around the corner from the velodrome, presumably waiting for a bus and still crying, red-eyed.

"Hey, hey!" he said, pulling her face close to his. "I wasn't trying to hurt your *feelings!*"

"Well, you *did*! And you better be *careful* with what you *say* to me, *Sam...*"

"Why don't you go home and rest?" he said. "That way, you'll be ready and prepared in case something happens. Like, say, that crazy girl actually comes *after* you..."

"Yeah. You're right. As usual," Jody answered, giving Sam a powerful hug that nearly broke his ribs, as Jody's hugs were prone to do. "I'm gonna go back to base and power down a bit. You have a rest, too, okay?"

"Sure. But walk, don't fly. Flying is just for superheroics, otherwise it's on the Q.T. Remember?"

"Yeah. Q.T. sounds good right now," Jody yawned.

They went their separate ways, not knowing how soon- and how dramatically-they would be reunited.

IV.

Having vanquished Jefferson Ball with her tongue (or so it seemed, anyway), Hamilton Pomeranian ascended the stairs of their apartment building- she lived only one floor above her friend, which had obvious advantages and disadvantages. She knew she had to get inside right away, before the muggers came out (although her military training served as a safeguard against this) and into bed before Jefferson also came home and demanded an audience with her, which usually happened if they had had a fight earlier in the day. Hamilton's plan for the rest of the evening, as she thought while fiddling her keys in the door, was simply to change out of her usual street attire and into more feminine sleepwear before hitting the sack. That was her plan. It was not executed.

Instead, when she opened her door, Hamilton was immediately surrounded by a group of diminutive, leathery-skinned, lizard-like beings dressed in body covering black suits. Hamilton recognized them immediately. They were *aliens*! And ones skilled in martial arts, as well, by the look of their costumes. Yet they had reckoned without the fact that she, too, had martial arts training. Which she now proceeded to demonstrate.

"I don't know how you *morons* got *in* here," Hamilton said, "but you're going *out* the same way you came *in*!"

So saying, the diminutive but powerful ex-soldier launched herself directly at the alien ninjas. She bellowed and sputtered the same pseudo-Asian gibberish still associated with martial arts in this future time as it was erroneously done in the past by the humans. This was because the only way most beings learned martial arts now was not from direct instruction in specialized schools, but through distorted and badly dubbed perversions in the form of very old "chop socky" movies from a now non-existent country called Hong Kong. Hamilton, whose interest in the form predated even her army training, was now a third degree black belt in every separate form of the arts available to her (for she, unlike others, had taken the time to not only tell them apart but to understand each of their strengths and weaknesses), and she proceeded to demonstrate her expertise by kicking and chopping each of her attackers into a corner, where they lay, motionless.

Though victorious, Hamilton was concerned, for she knew that her attackers would not stay comatose forever. Knowing Jefferson Ball's cell phone number by heart (though, more often, *Jefferson* was the one calling *her*), Hamilton called her friend for assistance, hoping she was available and *praying* she was sober enough to help her fight.

"Pick *up*, Jefferson!" Hamilton pleaded as she waited for the dial tone to conclude her summons. After what seemed to be an interminably long period, Jefferson responded at the other end.

"Y'ello?" said that worthy, who, to Hamilton's relief, was not nearly as stewed as usual.

"Jefferson!" Hamilton said tersely. "I need your *help*!"

"Who *is* this?"

" 'Who *is* this?' It's HAMILTON!"

"Hamilton *who*?"

"HAMILTON POMERANIAN! You know, your *best friend*! The one you spend most of your time with- and *with whom* you rack up big bills *I* have to pay off 'cause you *never* have money of your *own*!"

"Oh, yes. I *seem* to remember *somebody* by that name...I believe she said my being *dead* would be an *improvement* over how I'm living my life *now*..."

"*All right*!" Hamilton blustered, reading Jefferson's tone exactly. "I'M SORRY! Now, get down here from whatever *dive* you happen to be in and HELP ME! I got these alien ninjas in here. I don't know how they got in. I knocked 'em out, but they're not *down*..."

Jefferson caustically responded with loud, disbelieving laughter.

"Don't be *silly*, Hamilton!" she said between her disbelieving laughs. "ALIEN NINJAS? I never saw anything in my *life* like that, and you know how far *I've* travelled!"

"*Jefferson,* I'M SERIOUS!"

"You're seriously *drunk,* is what *you* are! *Trust* me- I've been there enough times to *know*!"

"How can you *say* that? After all we've been through together? All the times we saved each other's asses? All the times I lent you money- AND *YOU* NEVER PAID IT *BACK*!"

"Oh, ho! Just for *that*, you're on your *own*!"

"God *damn it*, Jefferson! You can't just- URK!"

The abrupt change is tone was the result of Hamilton's revived assailants ganging up on her, throwing her into a gunny sack, tying it up, and existing the room. The line, of course, went dead.

"Hamilton!" Jefferson snapped, shouting into the phone out of genuine concern for her friend's fate. "HAMILTON!" The genuine concern rose into genuine fear as she shut her cell phone. "HAMILTON!!!!" Rising from her booth at a local bar, she came to a definite conclusion.

"That *settles* it!" she shouted, seething with rage, about the hum of a group of patrons unaware of or uninterested in her words. "*Nobody* kidnaps Jefferson Ball's *best friend* without bringing upon them Jefferson Ball's *WRATH*! You *hear* me? NOBODY!!! Hang on, Hammy- I'M COMING!"

She rushed out of the tavern, slamming the door so hard that all of the glass in it shattered and broke- as did all the glasses, steins, mugs, crystal, china and everything else fragile in the place.

V.

Samuel Poodle's intent, as he returned to the small house he had inherited from his parents , was remarkably similar to Hamilton Pomeranian's- curl up in his plush, comfortable bed and go to sleep. Alas for him, like her, he found a stranger in his domicile when he arrived- one that, also like hers, was not of the Earth he knew.

He was a male dog like Sam himself, but there the similarities between them ended. The stranger's fur was white, as opposed to Sam's light gray, and he was both taller and more powerfully built than the

Hudson High cheerleader. This meant that Sam would likely lose if he chose to fight him- though Sam was not much of a fighting guy, anyway. But what was most odd to Sam was the stranger's dress- a cape, speedo and boots, all red, with a white "R" insignia prominently displayed on all of them. At first, Sam wondered if his reputation had preceded him, and that this was a member of his "tribe" (as Jody had called them) who was after the particular brand of "loving" only he could conceivably supply. But that idea quickly passed- Sam knew full well that his "kind" didn't advertise themselves *that* flamboyantly in public. Only beings who mocked them publicly, in the subtle racist fashion of the times, did *that*. So Sam decidedly to deal with this fellow purely based on what he clearly was: an invader of his personal sanctity.

"Who *are* you?" he demanded. "And *how* did you get into my *house*? I have a *deadbolt*!"

"I expected *that* from the likes of *you*," answered the stranger curtly. Then, in mocking stereotypical "gay" tones, he added: "Even though you've likely seen *some* royalty in your time, *huh*? Just not *me, sugar*- not 'til *now*!"

"And *you* are?" Sam prompted angrily.

"Remus The Twenty-Third," came the reply, as the stranger switched back to his normal, commanding heterosexual tone of voice. "I'm the King- KING, mind you- of a little plot of land way out there in the farthest regions of space. Some place that *you* could only *dream* of visiting!"

Sam, calling on his speed in place of his limited strength, tried to rush past Remus and escape him, but Remus caught him mid-sprint, and, with a powerful thrust, threw him backwards into a conveniently placed chair, from which the seemingly invincible monarch continued to pontificate down towards the secret agent/cheerleader, whom he clearly regarded as a *very* inferior being.

"I can come here to Earth whenever I damn well *please*," Remus continued, "thanks to some rips in the space time continuum that some dumb humans created back in the days when nobody knew what the hell they were *doing*! I know what *I* want, though- to take over EARTH! Granted, I've been *thwarted* every time I've tried to do it in the past, but, I swear to God, NOT THIS TIME!"

"And I'm supposed to *believe* that?" countered Sam. "A long winded monologue from a guy who only *claims* to be a "king", when he *easily* could *just* be a *professional wrestler* who can't get a steady *gig* anymore!"

"*DAMN* YOU TO *HELL, pal*!" Remus snarled back viciously. "Didn't I just *tell* you I was a *king*? Didn't that "Twenty Third" mean a damn *thing* to you? Y*eah*, I'm a *king*, and a damn *good* one, at that. *You* would be, too, if *you* had to live up to what *twenty two* guys with *your name* did *before* you! I don't have to take this kind of *crap* from a *swish* who goes around wearing a goddamn *SKIRT*!"

Sam's blood boiled, and his fur nearly turned purple, upon hearing this remark.

"If you're casting *aspersions* on my *doghood, sir,*" he snarled, "..then I suggest that you..."

He never completed the suggestion, for Remus grabbed his muzzle and began to squeeze it tightly.

"I don't need to hear any more *shit* out of *you*, you tail chasing *lemon squeezer*!" Remus said. "I hate *everything* you guys are and what you *stand* for! Hell, I made it *illegal* in my armed forces so I wouldn't have to look it in the *face*! And I wouldn't even have *crossed your threshold* tonight were it not for the fact that my *business partners* seem to look on you as a big wheel of some sort. So I'm taking you with me as a way of sealing the deal, you dig? But that doesn't mean I can't *personally* think of you as the walking pile of *slime* you are- or to *treat* you like it if I feel so inclined. Which I *do*!"

He threw Sam down on the floor and allowed him to gain his breath.

"Come on!" Remus ordered, motioning for Sam to rise. "We're late as it is, thanks to *you* being a stuck-up *jerk*- like all the guys in your "tribe" pretty much *are*. Get *up*, damn it!"

He kicked Sam in the skirt to emphasize his need for prompt compliance. After whining in obvious pain from the kick for a few seconds, Sam slowly rose up. In spite of the pain, however, Sam was still defiant, and his next words made that clear to Remus.

"I insist on my right to have one phone call before you ABDUCT me!" Sam said.

"Do I look like a COP to you?" retorted Remus.

"If you're after me for the reason I *think* you are," responded Sam, "then I have to let my *associate* know about it. You know, in case she wants to *liberate* me from your clutches, which I have no doubt that she will!"

"Whadaya mean, your...?" began Remus.

Then he stopped- and suddenly seemed to realize what Sam was getting at.

"Fine, *twist*!" Remus said. "Go ahead and *call* her. But first, I'm gonna tell you *what* to say- 'cause she needs to be where I *want* her to be for this whole thing to *work*! Here-use my phone! But you say *exactly* what I want you to say, understand? Or else I'll rip your skirt clean off of you and put my boots to you- and *not* in a way you're gonna *like*! Dig? And don't talk so damn *long*, either. I'm gonna get stuck with *roaming* charges for every damn call I *make* on your planet. Yeesh!"

So saying, he tossed his phone to Sam with a warning glare, and Sam, not wasting any time, called the phone number of his best friend.

*

After returning from her adventure on the tennis court, Jody Ryder carefully placed her tennis trophy- one among many- in a private glass chamber bedecked with her athletic prizes, in the equally private chamber at Fort Hugopolis where she resided when she was not on athletic or superhero duty. This being done, she yawned mightily, and then lay down in the special decompression chamber that allowed her to "sleep" while making sure that her body was recharged with energy in the interim, not unlike the sleep patterns of her "natural" colleagues. It pleased her that she could be "just like them" in this way.

Alas, the twelve hour slumber Jody had had in mind for herself was not to be. For, just over ninety minutes later, she was awoken- violently. One component of her robotic programming was a combination television/telephone concealed in her torso, which functioned the same as a cell phone in the outside world, except that it was only used between Jody and her colleagues at American Intelligence. Including- and especially- Sam.

As she vibrated, Jody sat bolt upright, opened her eyes, sighed deeply, and watched as the TV set emerged from out of her torso and pulled up to the level of her eyes. Sam, holding Remus' cell phone camera up to his face, appeared on the screen immediately.

"Jody!" Sam croaked nervously. "*Help*!"

"What the hell *is* it?" responded Jody. "Have you got your *toe* stuck in the *faucet* again?"

Her tone implied that using this communication system was a privilege that Sam had perhaps abused- more than once- in the past.

"Yuk, yuk!" Sam said sarcastically. "This time I'm *serious*!"

"What is it?" Jody asked, now concerned. "Are you in *trouble?*"

Sam's emphasis on the word "serious" was what convinced Jody because, for all his jocularity, Sam took his job seriously, more than even she did at times. And, though he had a tendency to exaggerate the status of problems he got himself into, he was very level headed in terms of an actual crisis, which is what this seemed to be right now.

"You might say that," Sam said in response to Jody's concerned questions. "It turns out that someone's broken into my house, and he..."

"Get *on* with it!" Remus hissed off camera.

"Well, why don't *you* talk to her, then?" said an annoyed Sam in response.

That got him a punch in the face from one of Remus' fists, as the other one pulled his cell phone towards his own visage.

"What the hell...?" Jody exclaimed as her friend's face was replaced by that of the stranger. "Who are *you*?"

Remus introduced himself, in the process displaying his typical immodesty by tacking on a large number of superlatives in addition to his name and number, hoping he might sway her feminine nature in his favor by boasting about his masculinity. It didn't work. After enduring as much of his posturing as she could stand, Jody vocally made her displeasure with him known.

"You *jerk*!" she spat. "You *better* leave Sam *alone* until I get to wherever it is you are, or *so help me...*"

"Ah! A *firecracker*!" Remus leered. "I know how to fix *your* type!"

"That won't wash, *scumbag!*" Jody shot back. "I'm a ROBOT!"

A thwarted Remus swore, loudly, violently and profanely. Once he controlled his temper, he continued addressing her.

"Well, maybe I can't hurt you the way I *want* to, but I can still *hurt* you!"

He took the camera off his face and pointed it back over onto a shiner-sporting Sam, miming firing a gun with his mouth as he did.

"You wouldn't DARE!" Jody roared.

"Think I *wouldn't?*" Remus said as he put the camera back on himself. "You want to save your *crush...*"

"He's *not* my BOYFRIEND!"

"...you get your metal plated ass over to the ruins of that old abandoned monastery outside of your town. And *pronto*, dig? Otherwise your *faggot* friend GETS IT!"

He signed off, and the screen went black, retreating into Jody's torso as it did. Opening her chest soon afterwards, Jody "upgraded" herself into her all powerful heroic form, waiting for the hatch in her room to open so she could fly out of it.

"When I get through with *you, Mr.* Remus The Twenty Third," she vowed, "the only thing you're going to be "king" of is YOUR LOUSY, PERVERTED *MIND*!"

With that, she took off out of the building to confront her newest enemy, and, as least she hoped, to prevail as she normally did.

VI.

Jody's departure from Fort Hugopolis was a quick one, as it usually was, and soon, to any observers who may have been on the ground that late at night, she was little more than a red, orange and white speck moving across the sky, like a hurricane on a meteorological monitor. Her hurrying was justified, though. Sam's safety- indeed, his very life- seemed to lay in the balance, and she needed to rescue him for him to escape further degradations at the paws of Remus. She had very much the intention not only to rescue him, but, with her typical relish in times of peak anger, to wipe the smile off Remus' face by busting his arrogant chops with her super-powered fists.

However, her rendezvous with Remus The Twenty Third would soon be unavoidably interrupted by someone with a desire to bust chops of her own.

Due to cold temperatures and a heavy layer of clouds, Jody was forced to fly above the clouds for much of her journey, nearly colliding with a jet in the process. After shaking a fist in anger at the retreating craft, Jody figured it would be better for her to fly low for the rest of the trip.

"I can't risk another collision," she said to herself. "Next time, broken pieces of *me* could fall from the sky!"

Fortunately, in retreating from the clouds, Jody discovered that her destination- the abandoned monastery- was now right underneath her, preventing her from needing to travel any further.

"Whew!" she said. "Exactly the spot he said. What luck!"

She zoomed down to Earth, and, taking the time to do a little private showboating, touched the Earth paws first, did a handstand and tumble, and then bowed and accepted thanks from an imaginary audience, giggling at her own audacity. Then she sobered up as the seriousness of her mission returned to her mind.

"Okay, *goofball*!" she ordered herself. "Get *serious*! You have a *duty* to do, and..."

Before she could continue reminding herself of her obligations, however, an enormous clump of dirt, nearly as big as Jody herself, came flying towards her. Not wasting a second, Jody quickly hit the dirt- by avoiding the clump through hitting the ground.

Outraged at this attempt on her life, Jody glared fiercely in the direction of where the clump of dirt had come from.

"All right!" she snapped angrily, like a school teacher nearly decapitated by a thrown eraser. "Who *threw* that?"

Silence.

"Come on- who *threw* that?"

Again, silence.

"I know you're *out* there, you *jerk*! You *hate* me- otherwise you wouldn't have *done* that! If you don't come out *right now,* I'll come in there and flush you out like the *rat* you are! You hear me? COME OUT!"

There was, yet again, no response for a moment. Then, suddenly, came a sharp retort.

"I'm a *rat*, huh? Okay, kid. You *asked* for it! You're going to meet your match *here and now* in the form of..."

Here, the voice interrupted itself to try to march out of a nearby cavern to a strain of triumphant music. Jody vaguely recognized the musical selection from one of the many films, videotapes and DVDs that had comprised her original programming, particularly from the beginning of one set of prints seen in succession. However, the intended processional was interrupted when the tape the figure using hit a snag and skipped over the part the mysterious figure intended to use.

"Hold it, hold it!" said the voice, accompanied by the sound of racing back to the tape machine in the cavern to fix the tape. "Got an issue here...hang on a second. Let me fix this here..."- here came the sound of the tape rewinding and the mysterious voice fixing it at the spot it wanted. "Okay- now, then! You're going to meet your match *here and now* in the form of..."

Here, the tape began again, and, at the triumphant end of the music composition, the owner of the voice strode out of the cavern and revealed herself in her full glory:

"JEFFERSON BALL!"

*

Once Jefferson emerged from the cavern where she had secluded herself, she strode, confidently, towards Jody, who had remained mute and somewhat stunned during Jefferson's audacious revelation, and who now stared at her in genuine confusion.

"*Well?*" Jefferson asked, poking Jody in the chest with an extended digit.

"Well, *what?*" Jody asked innocently.

"Aren't you going to get *mad* at me? I threw that clump of *dirt* at you, *didn't* I?"

"You did *not*! That was..."

"It *was* me!"

"That's *impossible*!" Jody flared. "It would take a creature with *more* than the strength of a *mere mortal* to throw something of the size and at the speed that that dirt clod came at me! *Much* more, in fact!"

Jefferson, upon hearing the words "mere mortal" seemingly directed at her, lost the easy jauntiness with which she had exited the cavern, and became genuinely outraged.

"How DARE you!" she stormed. "I am NOT a "mere mortal", as *you* seem to *think* I am! I, in fact, possess the strength to throw a clot of dirt in that quantity and shape, *and* the ability to throw said clot of dirt at the speed at which it came to you. In short, *I* THREW THAT GODDAMN PIECE OF *SOIL* AT YOU, you TIN-HEADED *LUNATIC*!"

"Don't *say* that!" bristled Jody. "There isn't a *single piece* of *tin* in my body! I'm entirely composed of an alloy of copper and..."

"SHADDAP!" barked Jefferson, with a finality that even Jody was intimidated by, as she took several steps backward from where Jefferson was standing. But Jefferson wasn't about to let her go. Pulling out her whip, she quickly let it fly.

The powerful strands caught around Jody Ryder's legs, and dropped her to the ground with a loud yelp before she could bat an artificial eyelid. Her quarry caught, Jefferson stood above Jody, forcing the latter to look up at her- reversing the earlier situation, when Jefferson was forced to look up at the robot. As Jefferson spoke, Jody now had no choice than to look up at her face- or what she could see of it, at that angle, that Jefferson's ample bosom wasn't blocking.

"All right now, girlfriend!" Jefferson said. "You and I are going to have a little *talk*!"

Jody didn't like the way Jefferson was talking right now- implicitly threatening her with physical and mental abuse for some imagined slight Jody had done to her, though they had never actually met before. And, while Jefferson had yet to demonstrate that she *did* possess the strength she claimed, if her muscle power matched her acumen with a whip, Jody wished to avoid a fight at all costs. If she was to rescue Sam from Remus, she needed to save as much of her strength as possible for that. So, in an attempt to placate Jefferson, she decided to play nice- up until when and if Jefferson decided to attack her.

"What about?" Jody asked, continuing to act as innocent as she was.

"Oh, just *girl* stuff," Jefferson said, faking (remarkably accurately) an innocent schoolgirl tone of her own. "Like *boys, dollys, tea parties,* our first *periods*- AND *YOU* STEALING ALL OF MY GODDAMN ATHLETIC RECORDS, YOU LITTLE *WITCH*!"

During this shift in vocal tone, Jefferson finally displayed the extent of her strength to Jody, raising her up off the ground and clean into the air with *one arm.* Jody was terrified. How, she now asked herself, was she to face this creature, who equalled her in strength- and was a *girl* like her, as well?

"I...don't know...what you're *talking* about!" Jody gasped, as she wiggled impotently in Jefferson's grasp.

"LIAR!" Jefferson blazed, throwing Jody to the ground with the same forceful strength she had used to raise her up. Then she forced her nemesis to stay in place by grasping, with that same powerful arm, one of Jody's own.

"I know *all about you, Ms.* Jody "I can't do a damn thing wrong 'cause I'm a *ROBOT*!" RYDER!" Jefferson continued. "I haven't *stopped* hearing about you since whenever the hell it was you came out of hiding, but ESPECIALLY after you started attending my sainted *alma mater*!"

"*You* went to *Hudson*?" Jody asked, successfully maintaining her innocence.

"DON'T CHANGE THE SUBJECT!" Jefferson growled, painfully strengthening her hold on Jody's arm as she did, to the robot's discomfort. "Hell *yeah,* I went to *Hudson!* In fact, I was one of the most *prestigious* students they ever had- *and* one of the most honored and *loved*! They said what I did would last *forever* in the record books. AND THEN *YOU* CAME ALONG!"

"What did I *do* that was so *wrong*?" Jody asked, still innocent.

"Didn't I just *tell* you that, *brat*? YOU BROKE MY *RECORDS*!"

"*What* records?" Jody asked, anger starting to fray her mask of innocence. "I don't know what you *mean*!"

"Then allow me to *enlighten* you. And to make sure you *hear me out...*"

With her free arm, Jefferson wound up and punched Jody in the face with all the strength at her command. Not only did she knock the robot into semi-consciousness, but she also dislodged parts of her artificial pelt from her body, making her existence as an artificial being even more plain to Jefferson. With Jody humbled temporarily, Jefferson released her hold on her arm and dropped her to the ground, standing over her as she began to speak again.

"Back in my younger days," Jefferson began, "which aren't as far away as *you* might *think*, I was, as I have already stated, the single most distinguished athlete Hudson High ever saw. That is, until *you* came along! But never mind *you*- this is about *me*! Maybe they wouldn't let me play *football* or *baseball* with the *boys,* like they somehow let *you* get away with, but any other sport they let me play, I *owned*. I scored more points in basketball, spiked more spikes than anyone ever could in volleyball, and beat the crap out of anybody who stood in my way on the field hockey pitch, while also scoring my fair share of goals *there* as well. But my pride and joy was being unmatched- *completely* unmatched!- in track and field. I ran long *and* short distances in record time. I chucked anything they tossed into my hands a country mile. *And* I jumped higher and longer than anyone else *dared*. And don't think it was *easy* for me to do all of those things, like it somehow is for *you*- 'cause it sure as hell WASN'T! Athletic training doesn't leave you much time for *boys* and *dating* and stuff like that! I missed out on that then- but I damn well sure made up for it as part of my *job*! Not to mention the fact that training does a big number on your *psyche*- but you, as a MACHINE, would know ZIP about that! No. I drove myself *hard* then to succeed, because I had nothing else going then. I wasn't what you would call a "brain", and I hadn't yet become the *boy magnet* I am now! It paid off when I set all of those records. I knew that I had accomplished something with them. Something that would last *forever,* and so, as a result, would *I.*"

"But *nothing* lasts *forever,*" interjected Jody.

"You would *know* that, WOULDN'T YOU?" Jefferson snarled. "You know how this all started? Hudson invited me to their last track meet so I could receive their Distinguished Alumnus Award- for all the *good* I've done in the world! It was *supposed* to be my crowning glory- being honored for *all* of my achievements by my sainted *alma mater*!"

"You should have been *proud* of that," Jody interjected again.

"Oh, I *was,* girl!" answered Jefferson. "I *was*! I say *was* because it was on that day that I saw *all* of my previously unassailable records *broken*! By YOU! *Every single one* of those precious things that defined me as a person, fueled my inner confidence and drive, taken away from me! It was if my *heart* had been ripped out of me and I was expected to just keep on *living*! I vowed I would make you *pay* for what you did to me- and when Jefferson Ball makes a vow, she doesn't goddamn half-step it, kid!"

"Since that time, I've been watching you at every damn athletic thing you've done. I can't *stand* that you've done all I've done *better* than me- *and* that they let *you* get away with a whole bunch of *crap* they never would have let *me* get away with! Oh, I've *been* there, honey! I get *drunk* and insult you and catcall you and do everything I can do to get you to *notice* me, but they always throw me *out* before I can get anywhere *near* you! *Not this time, sister*! I've got you now, and I'm *not* letting you *go* until we finally fight it out, girl to girl, to see which of us is *really* the *best*! And I know for *sure* that, record books be *damned,* it'll always be ME!"

During Jefferson's tirade, Jody Ryder's strength had finally returned to her. And so, just as Jefferson finished speaking, Jody spryly regained her feet, in the process towering over Jefferson again. She had also regained her incendiary teenage anger, unfortunately for Jefferson.

"Lady, you're *insane!*" Jody spat, as her canine ears flattened in anger. "You can't *possibly* hold *me* to account for running a bit faster or throwing something a bit farther than *you* did YEARS AGO! I have *no control* over what constitutes a record, and *neither do you!* If you have a hang-up about your "glorious" past, you're *living* in the past, and deluding yourself with your own self-centered *elitism!* It's your *own* fault you're as *screwed up* as you are, not *mine!* Now, I don't have time for *any more* of your *nonsense!* My *friend* has been *abducted* by *aliens,* and I have to *save* him! So get out of my way and get out of my *face-* FOREVER!"

Jody tried to walk away from Jefferson, in preparation for flying away from her, but Jefferson blocked her path.

"Didn't you *hear* me?" Jody roared. "I said..."

"I *heard* you, Ryder!" Jefferson roared back. "I got a pal in Dutch with aliens, too- but *that* can *wait!* You're probably in *league* with whoever took her, anyway, so if I get *you...*"

"How DARE you!" Jody answered. "I'm a HERO! I don't *do* those things! I can't say the same for *you,* though."

"WHAT?" Jefferson snapped. "I am *100% hero material!*"

"100 *proof aged,* more like it!" Jody said as she inhaled the alcohol on Jefferson's breath. "For all *I* know, *you* and that *alien king* I talked to earlier could be collaborators, too- and *you're* holding my friend *captive* to satisfy your own *sick sexual urges!*"

"You've *seen* what I can *do, robot!*" Jefferson said, balling her fists. "You want *more* of it?"

"I can take *anything you got,* you *drunken HAS-BEEN!*" Jody Ryder stormed back as she balled her own robot fists for the upcoming fight. "*More,* if I *have* to!"

"Then *so be it!*" pronounced Jefferson.

Once again, Jefferson delivered a roundhouse punch to Jody Ryder's face that left the robot reeling and sprawled on the ground. Yet Jody was not that easily defeated. When she got to her feet again-within seconds this time- she ran, screaming violently, towards Jefferson. Jody intended to deliver a knockout punch of her own, but Jefferson caught her arm and held her tight before the robot could do any such thing. Jody found herself again encased in Jefferson's vise-like grip, which now seemed impossible for even her to break.

"Let...me...GO!" Jody stammered as she struggled in Jefferson's grip.

"All right!" Jefferson said, deceptively calm. "If you *insist*!"

She picked Jody up again, held her above her head, and threw her around in a circle for a couple of minutes before dropping her on the ground again. Furious, Jody desperately sought parity with her new nemesis by cocking the powerful gun concealed in her left arm and aiming at Jefferson.

"THAT *DOES* IT!" the robot exploded. "I normally observe a no-kill rule in my protocol, but, *IN YOUR CASE*, I'll make an *EXCEPTION*!"

A high powered bullet came out of Jody's exposed gun aimed at Jefferson, but the latter dropped to the ground just in time. Still, she knew exactly what was going on.

"*Cheater*!" Jefferson snapped.

"Don't *call* me that!" answered an indignant Jody.

"I'll call you that if I *want* to," said Jefferson as she marched towards a nearby, thick-trunked tree. "*And*, if *you're* going to cheat on *your* ethical diet, I will on *mine*, too!"

Jefferson proceeded to uproot the giant tree by its roots easily, much to Jody's horror. Nevertheless, the robot was well aware of the fact that she needed to defend herself to survive this potentially lethal encounter, and she did. As Jefferson wielded the tree's trunk like a sword, Jody, armed only with her fists, deflected every blow aimed at her by punching through the tree's bark. After several of these blows in succession, Jody found her patience once again ebbing. With a final, super powerful punch, she smashed the tree into thousands of individual bits of wood, in the process knocking a stunned Jefferson backwards several feet onto her rump. With quicksilver speed, Jody rushed forward, grabbed Jefferson by the top of her pelt, and sternly gazed down upon her, seemingly the victor.

"I *believe* I've made my *point,*" Jody said. "I'll let you *live- if* you promise never to *bother* me AGAIN!"

"Think *otherwise,* GOODY TWO SHOES!" retorted Jefferson.

Before Jody could respond, Jefferson snaked her legs around the robot's and wrapped her powerful arms around her neck. Drop kicking Jody by pulling her legs forward and sending her falling to the ground, Jefferson then grabbed one of the robot's arms and forced her to start hitting *herself* in the face.

"Quit *hitting* yourself!" Jefferson repeated, in her mocking schoolgirl tone.

She repeated this in the same tones several additional times as she manipulated Jody's powerful fist towards her vulnerable face. This only served the purpose of reigniting the robot's vicious anger. Finding the strength to free herself from Jefferson, Jody violently punched her tormentor in her own face- so she would know exactly what that *felt* like! This sent Jefferson to the ground, at which point Jody grabbed her firmly in preparation for a second- and, hopefully, fatal- punch.

"I have *HAD* IT WITH YOU!" the robot thundered at her opponent, clearly intending to show Jefferson that she was as merciless as she was- and succeeding. "You leave me absolutely *no choice* but to ELIMINATE you!"

"Give it a *rest,* Ryder!" said an unfazed Jefferson. "Why don't just admit that I'm *better* than you, and leave it at that?"

"*NEVER!*" an unsympathetic Jody blazed back as she raised a fist towards Jefferson. "*I* am a force for all that is *good* in the world, and YOU are NOT!"

"Wanna *bet*?" taunted Jefferson.

This was the last nail in the coffin for Jody Ryder. She had *tried*, with all her might, to reason with this creature who was as feminine as she was, and claimed to be a "hero", besides, but it wasn't working. At this point, everything that was humane, sympathetic and organic within her was swiftly destroyed, leaving her only with the hollow metal exterior of the heartless machine she only appeared to be to face Jefferson. And nothing epitomized this better than the vicious desire to *kill* she now felt, to the detriment of her programming.

Throwing words aside, Jody roared like a dragon as she enclosed both of her powerful paws around Jefferson's neck, intending to squeeze the life out of her as quickly as possible. But Jefferson was a battle scarred veteran herself, and knew that trick well. Just as Jody began wrapping her paws around her neck, Jefferson threw her own powerful arms in a similar embrace around *Jody's* neck, creating a vicious battle to the death in the process.

The rest, as the saying goes, is history. After breaking each others' holds on their necks, Jefferson and Jody reverted to the nature of the battles that had been fought by their wild ancestors (or, at the very least, Jefferson's.) Barking, growling, snapping, snarling and cursing, they tackled each other, wrestled each other to the ground, rabbit punched each other, and otherwise fought each other in the most unladylike of ways, though both had long since thrown *that* particular protocol out the window. Jody bit Jefferson hard with her fangs, and Jefferson, unable to respond in kind due to Jody's metal skeleton, responded by tearing any bit of Jody's artificial pelt she could reach off of her. They picked up rocks, grass, soil, trees, plants and anything else they could find at each other, but, as always, the other one ducked just in time to avoid the thrown missives. For a finale, they clamped each other's arms and legs around their bodies and plainly wrestled, though both remained upright through the process and neither "dropped" the other as planned. But the effects were felt by others in other ways. Residents of the nearby hill country around Hugopolis swear to this day that an earthquake was felt in the area the night of the fight, although the community is not on any fault line or plate of the Earth whatsoever.

The battle might have continued indefinitely, but, after another half-hour, the same black clad aliens who had kidnapped Hamilton Pomeranian secretly emerged from behind on the pair. Without further notice, they produced electrical charges in their fingertips and touched the gladiators, electrocuting Jefferson Ball, short circuiting Jody Ryder, and rendering them both unconscious. Marshaling their own, more limited, strength, they picked up the powerful females and removed them from the field of battle.

VII.

His eyes covered by a blindfold, Samuel Poodle, jammed from behind with sharp sticks, was ushered into a prison cell cautiously, so that he would not stumble and accidentally fall on the floor. This was because his captors had been sternly advised by their leader *not* to purposely damage him because of his extreme value to them. Consequently, Sam- *after* Remus The Twenty Third had casually knocked him out following their *tete-a-tete* with Jody Ryder- had been blindfolded and only revived when he arrived at the base of operations Remus and his "men" shared with their fellow alien race to engage in what they hoped would be a successful attempt to conquer the Earth. As a result, it was not until Sam was safely inside the cell- and the blindfold removed from his eyes- that Remus' "men" felt free to taunt Sam for his "girly" manner and dress. This, of course, made him livid, but they escaped his wrath by firmly shutting the cell door in front of him after running out of the doorway. This had the unpleasant effect of making Sam crash into the cell door and fall down to the hard dirt floor below.

Holding a paw to his head in pain, Sam uttered an ugly, wordless groan to express the extent of how physically hurt he was. This only to served to attract the attention of his cellmate, who uttered:

"Well! Hello, there!"

That being was, as you might have guessed, Hamilton Pomeranian. After being abducted by her own captors, she had gone through the same routine as Sam, although he, at least, had been spared the indignity of being stuffed into a gunny sack. She had emerged from the experience embittered at her captors, and she no doubt believed Sam felt the same way- *if* he was willing to talk to her about it, to begin with. Until then, her ability to escape seemed unlikely without a confederate. And, seeing as her usual confederate was MIA, she would have to improvise.

Cautiously, Hamilton came towards Sam.

"You hurt?" she asked.

"What does it *look* like?" he answered caustically. "I took about a *pound* of metal on my *head*!"

"I wasn't trying to *offend* you," she responded calmly. "God knows, I took *that* kind of punishment when I was in the star soldiers *all* the *time*! The important thing is knowing how to *survive* it!"

"*You* were in the *star soldiers*?" Sam said with disbelief. "You're so...."

"I know where you're *going, Klinger*," she growled, "and I don't *like* it!"

"*Watch it* with that kind of talk!" Sam responded, getting to his feet, at which point he towered over Hamilton, though it did not faze her at all. "I don't take kindly to *it,* either!"

"Then let's agree to disagree," Hamilton rumbled. "*You* don't make any cracks about me being short, *or* me having a bum eye, *or* me having a gimpy walk..."

"I never even *mentioned*..."

"And *I* won't make any cracks about you being a skirt wearing SISSY!"

Sam bit his lip. Being a sissy was...slightly..better than being a faggot, homo or pussyfoot, which is what he was *used* to being called by rivals and unsympathetic strangers. So this....female...obviously wasn't as prejudiced against him for what he was, in spite of her angry tone. That was good. At least he could *try* to approach her on her own terms. But there was a complication. For why, out of all of the myriad different feelings he *could* possibly have about her, was he now somewhat *attracted* to her- *physically*? Fortunately, he could, also surprisingly, see that *she* felt the same way about *him,* particularly noticing the misgivings with the idea she seemed to have in her eyes. Yet they decided, for the time being, to try to ignore the elephant in the room.

"We...uh...haven't been properly introduced," Hamilton said, extending a paw to him, which he took and shook. Hamilton identified herself with her name, rank and serial number, and he promptly identified himself as an agent of American Intelligence, saluting her as he did.

"Never mind *that*!" Hamilton responded. "I'm *retired*! And even when I *was* on active duty, I never liked that BS too much, anyway. Folks who do that crap just want to rise as fast in the ranks as they can so that the *grunts* don't get *dirt* on them. Not me. I was happy to just *be* there, seeing as I wasn't exactly an A Prime specimen of canine humanity, even *before* I got my infirmities. But, at the same time, I knew my place and I *stayed* there. Because I had to keep the line moving, so to speak. Now, my friend Jefferson Ball..."

Jefferson Ball? Not *the* Jefferson Ball? The heroine of Earth- and a thousand other planets besides! In spite of his own universe trotting in the company of Jody Ryder, Sam still felt as star struck as anyone else on Earth would be to be even *acquainted* with somebody who, however tenuous it might be, even knew in passing *the* Jefferson Ball. Sam did not say anything of these things to Hamilton, but he still made his feelings about Jefferson known to her by allowing his mouth to gape- wide- at the mention of her name. Hamilton caught the reference, and, with some effort given the disparity in their sizes, managed to shut his maw again. What she said next to him shattered his illusions.

"You've *heard* of her, have you?" Hamilton said, sarcastically. "But nary a peep about *me,* right?"

Sam nodded reluctantly.

"It's okay," Hamilton answered. "I'm not surprised. I haven't gotten a lick of press since my soldiering days, but I'm used to anonymity. Kind of nice, actually. But what I *don't* like is the fact that *Ms. Glory Hog* likes to pretend like she accomplishes everything she does *single handed-* when it's actually *me* who does a fair share of the dirty work *for* her. ME! Not that I care about the lack of attention. But she can just be such a goddamn IDIOT sometimes! I mean, she wouldn't still be *alive* today if I hadn't had to *save* her in the nick of time- like I usually *have to do*! She wouldn't be able to drink as much liquor and bed as many boys as she does if *I* didn't make sure she has the cash and the rubbers she needs for both of those things- which she *never reimburses* me for! And whatever success she has had in *business* is entirely *my* doing- 'cause she sure as hell doesn't know a damn thing about *money!* Honestly! Lock her up in a room with money, boys and liquor and she'd *never* want to come out. Me, I try to think *beyond* that."

"I know what you mean," Sam said, sympathetically. "Not easy being a second banana, is it? Try being a straight man for a *robot* sometime. A robot who could *tear you apart* if she wanted to!"

"Oh, *Sam*uel! You have no need to explain that to *me*. I'm as well acquainted with the exploits of *Miss* Jody Ryder as anybody could be!"

"You're talking about the sports stuff, right?"

"Yep. And the *other* stuff, too."

"WHAT?"

"Now, don't get so upset!"

"What Jody does when she's a superhero- and what I do *with* her- is *not* supposed to be public knowledge! People are *not* supposed to know that she...."

"...is a *superhero*. Look, Sam. You've been a good boy. You and Jody have managed to hide the reasons *why* you go on those missions, haven't you?"

"Yeah, but...."

"BUT- you *cannot* expect to have Jody go and do what she does and *not* have people know that she *did* it. Not in this day and age. Somebody's always going to be recording you when you don't expect them to- and *then* they'll play the tape back in your face like some sort of *aural shit* to rub your face in and *discredit* you. Trust me on this. I was a government employee long before you were."

"So you're saying other people know...and have seen me and her....AAAAAHHHHH!"

"Relax!" It was a command, so Sam did as she told him. "All I'm saying is that it was reported on, not necessarily that it was *filmed*. The same way Jody's sporting events got reported on and distributed to the world after she completed her performances." She took a big, rueful breath and sighed. "And *that* is how I got into this mess!"

"What "mess"?" Sam asked suspiciously.

"My pal Jefferson is out to kill your pal Jody. And, knowing her, she won't stop until she *does*!"

"WHAT????"

"Didn't I tell you to RELAX? Do you want the guards to come in here and *beat* us or something? I've already been *through* that today, pal, and you have, too, from the looks of you. It won't be good for *either* of us to go through it *again*! So just clam up and COOL IT!"

Sam nodded, mutely. It was all he could do under the torrent of her words.

"All right," Hamilton continued, calmly. "Here's the deal about all of this. Jefferson is an alumnus of the same school you and Jody go to in your "civilian" lives. Jody *happened* to break some of the records Jefferson set, as well as getting some of the opportunities Jefferson, for all her trying, never got. Like playing football, for instance."

"Jody's *good* at that."

"Is she *ever*! But that's not the point. Jefferson has been seeing green ever since J.R. arrived in town, and she's hell bent on converting your pal into scrap iron. And she's strong and mean enough to do it. Trust me!"

"I know. I saw a picture of her decapitating a robot bigger than Jody with *one punch* in the paper once."

"That was a fake. It never happened."

Sam's mouth gaped again.

"She does that kind of stuff all the time. Half of the "legendary" stuff she does is really puff pieces like that. Which she pays for mostly with *my* money, *thank you very much!*"

Sam's mouth remained agape.

"Did I *disillusion* you, there, son?"

"She *fakes* everything she *does*?" Sam retorted, appalled.

"Not *all* of it! *And*, I'll *remind* you, she was saving the world from evil long *before* Jody and yourself came around! I can testify to that. At least for the times I was around to "help" her. The times I *wasn't* around, I can't tell if she's B.S.-ing or not."

"But *why* would she feel the need to pad her resume with stuff she never did? Jody would *never* think of taking credit for things she didn't do. It's just not in her mindset!"

"Well, there we have the essential difference between Ms. Ryder and Ms. Ball. Jefferson, for one thing, has an *ego. You* would have one, too, if you were as fast and strong as she is at peak operating power. But, underneath it all, she's kind of insecure. She thinks boys are only attracted to her because she supposedly can whip her weight in wildcats across the universe and back, and so she exaggerates herself and her abilities so she can nail as many as she can when she feels frisky. Usually, she *drinks* when she makes those boasts, too, and *anybody* is bound to exaggerate things when they get *drunk*. It's happened to *me,* and I've lived to *regret* it. You drink, Sam?"

"No!" He was appalled in tone, but he was also now fighting a desire to get into her pants, a previously foreign feeling for him. Just like she was clearly, in both tone and words, fighting in vain to reveal her desire to get beneath his skirt.

"Good fellow. And, of course, Jody doesn't, either."

"Yes, she does. Motor oil."

"But that doesn't have *alcohol* in it."

"Right."

Hamilton took off her dashiki and whipped it in front of her face like a fan.

"Is it just me, Sam," she asked, "or is it getting *hot* in here?"

"It's....not   just....you,....Major,"   Sam   confessed.   "I   don't normally..."go"   for   girls,   but   something   about you...is...doing....*something to*...me!"

"And I know what that "something" is, boy! C'mere!"

He did. When he arrived, Hamilton gripped his paws and spun him towards the wall. She had to stand on the tips of her boots to kiss him, so great was the difference in their heights. But Sam made up for that by scooping the bottom part of her body in his right arm so the difference between their mouths would not be as vast. However, before they could proceed to more sexually explicit activity, they were interrupted by a torrent of sound and activity on the other side of the wall-one marked by particularly angry language from both sides of a conversation.

"You hear that?" Hamilton asked.

"Yeah," said Sam. "That sounds like *Jody*!"

"And *Jefferson*!" Hamilton added.

They pressed their ears to the wall to hear what was going on.

VIII.

What had happened, a few minutes earlier, was that Jefferson Ball and Jody Ryder, both with arms and legs tightly bound (for safety's sake), Jefferson unconscious and Jody inoperative, were brought to the joint headquarters of their respective enemies- Remus The Twenty Third (Jefferson's) and the little green alien ninja lizards (Jody's). Each villainous assemblage had failed to defeat the heroine opposing them multiple times in the past. Aware that they shared the same goals, for their planets were only mere light years apart, they had decided to kill several birds with one stone- conquer the Earth *and* their enemies at the same time. By not attacking their usual foes, capturing the respective sidekicks of their new opponents, and, especially, by manipulating the heroic duo into seeing each other as their enemy- resulting in their recent, destructive, near-battle to the death- the villains had now come as far as they could towards gaining their goal. So far.

With this in mind, Remus and his counterpart, Flebus, seated in opposing chairs in the center of the room, where they were both surrounded by their loyal, fawning flunkies, were well prepared to receive the entrance of their defeated foes. When the humbled heroes were escorted in, therefore, they grinned like twin Cheshire Cats as soon as they saw them.

The leaders walked down towards their captives. After admiring them in their impotent glory for a few seconds, Remus expressed the view of the majority when he said:

"All right! Wake 'em up!"

His order was acted upon. Jefferson was slapped into consciousness, while, through trial and error, Jody was brought back online.

Their first sight on revival was each other, and, with wordless growls, they tried to lunge for each other, but their bonds were too tight and they didn't yet possess the strength to free themselves. Remus further short-circuited their aim to fight again by motioning two of his "men" wordlessly to hold them in place. Flebus did the same with two of his operatives, so they were surrounded on all sides.

"That'll be *enough* of *that*!" Remus pronounced, imperiously. "You two have spent enough time *as it is* fighting tonight. You *totally* wore out the *batteries* on our *cameras*! *Panavision film* doesn't grow on *trees*, you know!"

"Shut *up*!" Flebus interjected. "They weren't supposed to *know* that!"

"Well, they do now," Remus observed, ruefully. "My bad."

"*Cameras*?" said Jefferson angrily.

"You were *filming* us?" added an outraged Jody.

"Damn right we were," said Flebus. "You can't make a "fight of the century" DVD without getting the footage you *need* for it!"

"So you *conned* us into *fighting* each other?" Jefferson asked.

The monarchs nodded.

"And that whole thing about capturing our *best friends* was just a ruse to get us to *fight for you*?" added Jody.

Again, the monarchs nodded.

"How DARE you!" exploded the robot. "We are NOT for *sale*! Our heroic abilities and activities are *not* for you to *profit* from!"

"Darn right they're not," added Jefferson. "They're for *us* to profit from! I can't *believe* you were going to market me and copper-bottom here duking it out for public consumption- and *not* give me any share of the *profits!*"

"JEFFERSON!" roared a furious Jody Ryder. "Is *that* all you can *think* of right now? The *money* you could make? Our *reputations* are at *stake* here!"

"Look," Jefferson said calmly to Jody. "I wasn't gonna stiff ya, *Robocop*! I'm a good negotiator! You'd get the same share of the kitty as me- I'd make *sure* of it!"

"YOU..." Jody exploded.

She was aroused now, and wanted to smash Jefferson in her face for her contemptible, arrogant behavior. But she was held in check by her captors, and prevented from further attacking Jefferson., who was now expressing a similar desire to wipe away Jody's sweetness-and-light mentality by punching *her* in the face, but she was likewise held in check.

"You seem to hate each other now as much as Remus and myself hate you both individually," observed Flebus. "That's only going to make the final cut of the DVD more *authentic*!"

"Yuk it up all you want, *guys*," Jody snapped. "But you can be damn well sure that I'll get out of this trap and find *all* of those *rotten cameras* and *destroy* them before you can assemble an *answer print*! And *when I do*..."

"Oh! *Really*!" answered Jefferson, in a bitchy tone. "*You're* just mad that I *beat* you!"

"You....LOUSY...*ONE-UPMANSHIP ARTIST!*" blazed Jody in response.

She sent a beam of light from her eyes that hit Jefferson on her exposed torso and made her shout and curse in pain loudly, unable to fight back. For good measure, Jody then turned her head as much as she could towards the monarchs.

"And *you,* you two *third-rate HITLERS!*" she stormed. "I'll give it to *you* worse than I will *her* when I get *out* of here!"

Another blast of light from her eyes, and a jet of flame from her mouth, shot out at the monarchs, who ducked just in the nick of time. Flebus, who was used to Jody's teenage impertinence, merely glared angrily at the robot and said nothing, but Remus, who was not as familiar with her antics as he was with Jefferson Ball's, was genuinely frightened, shocked, angered and appalled by her actions- all at once. Acting quickly, as he was accustomed to doing, he ordered his "men" to use duct tape to seal Jody's mouth, and then to place an iron bucket over her head. Both of these actions were undertaken so that Remus would not have to look at Jody's "arrogant" face any further, and also to prevent her making any more attempts on either his life or Flebus'. She couldn't aim her weapons at them if she couldn't *see* them, after all.

When Jefferson, with typical bad timing, proceeded to laugh raucously in response to Remus' decision to humble her rival, this did not sit well with the King, Emperor, Viceroy and All-Around Homewrecker of the Commonwealth of Remula (to give his full title). With murder in his eyes, he determined to punish his long-time enemy for her devilish impudence. From the pocket of his cape, he withdrew a portable branding iron he kept for emergencies such as this, lit a match on it, and then firmly and sadistically placed his brand- a giant "R"- on her navel.

"*Nobody* laughs at me!" he snarled. "Especially not *you*, you filthy old ball-busting COW!"

She swore violently at him in response, and, to answer her, he ordered his "men" to bind *her* lips with duct tape as well. Which they did post-haste.

Just then, one of Remus' aides informed him that the first "cut" of the Jefferson/Jody fight was now ready for his inspection.

"Hah!" the dog king snapped at the humbled Jody Ryder. "Here's your "answer print" NOW, you mechanical SLUT!!!"

He then turned to his and Flebus' aides, surrounding them both and waiting for further instruction.

"Come *on,* already!" Remus ordered, impatiently. "Get the screen and projector ready. Let's ROLL this *garbage!*"

They proceeded to do exactly as he commanded.

"I get to make suggestions and changes, right?" Flebus asked Remus while their aides went about their work. "Otherwise I don't know *what* I'm doing here!"

"Of course," Remus assured him. "If you don't like anything in the print, you can cut it from your version. These are just the rushes, understand? But we'll make *another* print for you to cut. *This* print is *my bitch*! Remember our deal. You get distribution rights for the eastern universe, and I get 'em for the western universe. And *never* the twain shall *meet*. Or *else*!"

He made a cutting motion across his throat with one "finger" to emphasize the potential consequences of going against their deal.

"That's all well and good," Flebus said. "Provided *you* do the same."

"Do you *still* not *trust* me?" Remus responded, rolling his eyes and throwing up his paws.

"I don't trust *anyone*," Flebus answered. "How do you think we stay *alive* as a race?"

"Good point," Remus said. "*I* don't trust anyone, *either*, by the way. For the same reason."

They eyed each other warily, until they were told that the film was ready for viewing, and ambled off to their respective chairs to watch it. Jefferson and Jody, meanwhile, were kept under restraints, so they could do nothing to stop the film from being shown. For the moment.

After the obligatory numbered leader, the logos of the two villains' production companies appeared on the screen. First came the alien ninjas' logo, which consisted of a glistening blue marble of a planet-their own home world- surrounded by wispy rings, against a thick, black, star bedecked sky. In the middle of the screen, printed in front of the planet, was the legend...

From

ALIEN NINJA LIZARDS

A Republican Party Company

...accompanied by a short orchestral "sting" provided by an orchestra and synthesizer.

Following a transitional "AND", on a blank black screen, Remus' logo appeared. It consisted of a bright, daylight sky, at the top of which, dead in the center, was the single majestic word:

REMUS

...in enormous capital letters. Beneath that was what appeared to be Remus himself, outfitted in a toga, laurel wreath, and sandals, holding a torch in his left paw, whose light dominated the image, and a tablet under his right paw. Beneath this tableau was a smaller legend:

REMUS TWENTY THREE INDUSTRIES
A UNIT OF THE CONSERVATIVE PARTY OF CANADA

This was also accompanied by an orchestral "sting", also this one had no synthesizer on it.

This ID now over, the narrative proper of the film began, following the appearance of the title- "BITCH SLAP OF THE MILLENIUM-RYDER VS. BALL"- in letters of red that appeared to be dripping blood. From that point on, the fight as it has already been detailed unspooled, with the exception of the fact that, through close-ups, reaction shots, trick shots from a variety of angles, and sophisticated but unsubtle uses of cinematography and editing, it was made even more nasty, brutish and uncivilized than it actually was. Remus, Flebus and their vassals watched the film in the boorish, uncivilized fashion of Canadian hockey fans, making copious comments on the "plays" going on, and reacting, as expected, to gratuitously inserted images of Jefferson and Jody's mammaries and *tuchuses*, many of which involved them being grabbed and manhandled. It was clear to whom this film was going to be marketed towards, and, indeed, how its marketers were inclined to view the Ms.s Ryder and Ball, now and in the future.

When it was all over, the film was rewound, and, on Remus' orders, returned to the safety of the film library. At this point, he swaggered forth to address his captives.

"Great job, girls!" he said. "Fabulous! We got a real *blockbuster* here! Me and the lizard guys are going to make a *mint* on this! And the best thing about it is that, after it drops, you two *tramps* will never be able to show your *faces* in the universe *again*! But stick around- we'll probably need to you to do some *retakes* later on!"

The leer with which he uttered the word "retakes", and the evil laugh that accompanied the whole speech, made it clear to both Jefferson and Jody how much of a pickle they really were both now in, and gave them much to think about after Remus ordered them removed from his sight just after that.

IX.

Jefferson and Jody were hustled off to a small, cramped cell located in an anteroom off from the central area of the headquarters. Once inside, their restraints were removed, the bucket removed from Jody's head, and the duct tape was removed from both of their mouths- violently. The soldiers guarding them then took their leave and shut the door behind them.

"Any chance of them getting out?" one asked as they left.

"No *way*!" said another. "This thing has a lock tighter than a drum. Besides, they hate each other so much that they'll probably *kill* each other, anyhow. We'll find their *corpses* in the morning!"

Once alone, Jefferson and Jody briefly considered fighting again, but both were too tired and frustrated now for such a concentrated effort. Instead, they slumped down into opposite sides of the cell, for the time being. They chose, instead, to try to sleep to regain their strength. But, after about twenty minutes of this attempt, Jefferson awoke upon hearing something suspicious.

"Hey!" she shouted. "ROBOT! Wake up!"

"I have a *name*, you know!" Jody responded, petulantly.

"Okay, *Jody*! I think they're getting copies of that film ready to send 'round. We better get up and at 'em if we want to..."

"*WE?*" the robot screamed, with sizzling hot acid in her voice. "*WE?*"

"Uh, *yeah*!" Jefferson said, as if talking to a child. "It's the plural form of "I"- as in you and myself...."

"I *KNOW* WHAT IT *MEANS*!" retorted Jody. "What I *can't* understand is *why* you want to *work* with me now- when you were only *hours* ago trying to *kill* me?"

"Oh, for the love of MIKE!" Jefferson shouted. "Are you still *sore* about that? You're giving me too hard a time about..."

"I have EVERY REASON TO!"

"Look, *Terminator*! The *only* reason you and I were scrapping was because we each thought the other guy took our best friend. Which is *bullshit*! You and I were *both* played like a couple of country rubes by our city slicker alien enemies! And what we did to each other is going to be the toast of every planet in the universe. And our reputations as heroes *and* as "women"- whatever *that* is- is going to be exactly the same thing- *toast*! That is, if we *don't* liberate our pals, destroy *all* the prints of that glorified stag reel, and plant our enemies in the dirt with a couple of one-twos!"

"And why should *I* trust *you*? You insulted my femininity..."

"You're a ROBOT!"

"...ridiculed my reputation, made me the scapegoat for the *death* of *your youth,* honored *your* athletic achievements at the expense of my own, and made me feel inadequate, weak and helpless simply for being a *robot.* You should be *ashamed* of yourself! Don't expect me to *forgive* you for what you *did* to me- because I have absolutely NO intention of doing ANY SUCH THING!"

"*All right!* Would it help if I said I was sorry?"

"No!"

"If I said I was acting my own anger out at your expense?"

"No!"

"If I said I was foolish, stupid and headstrong for doing that- and you were, too?"

"*Not* helping!"

"What if I offered to take you to the car wash? Take you for a lube job? Shack you up with a guy robot?"

"ABSOLUTELY *NOT*!"

"God *damn* it!" shouted Jefferson. "Who the hell *programmed* you, anyway? The VICTORIANS?"

"I have a very firmly defined sense of right and wrong," Jody answered. "There's *no* ambiguity in the way I see the world. Anyone who does good to me is good and is my friend, and anyone who does bad to me is my enemy. Guess which one YOU are!"

"Guess what, kid?" Jefferson responded. "*You* may work that way, but the *real world* sure as hell *doesn't*! People you think are good might stab you in the back, and people who seem bad *might* go a long way to help you if they thought it might benefit both of you. Consider *me* in *that* position *right now*. We may *despise* each other right now, it's true, but that's only because we got off on the wrong foot. The number we did on each other could easily be unleashed on the ones we should *really* be hating. Remus, king of the ASSHOLES, is somebody I've kicked the crap out of before, and I'd *gladly* do it again. You've kicked Flebus and his glorified geckos around, too, by the looks of it, and you'd hurt 'em just as hard if you wanted to. *And* we have to save our pals, still. So give me a *chance* here, Jody. Will ya?"

Jody sighed and rolled her eyes.

"All right," she said. "*One* chance. *But*, if you even *try* to sock me *again*, I'll *kill* you! Now- you have a plan?"

"Yeah."

"Let's hear it."

*

The plan was simple enough. They both knew full well that Remus's soldiers were correct when they said the door to their cell was impenetrable. To test their assumptions, they both threw super-powerful fists at the door. Despite their joint power, the door barely moved when each threw a punch separately, as well as when they did it together. So another solution to their dilemma had to be found. This was the essence of Jefferson's plan.

"They're expecting us to try to escape," Jefferson said. "That's why they made the door out of whatever the hell it is they made it out of. So we couldn't get out that way. They think they stopped us cold by doing that. But they *didn't*. There are *other* ways for us to escape."

"Such *as*?" Jody prompted. "I don't see any *windows* in here- or any *other* kinds of air or light distribution systems we could possibly *squeeze* through!"

"Look down," Jefferson continued.

Jody did- and suddenly understood what Jefferson meant.

"Are you *serious*?" Jody said, with rhetorical anger.

"What's the *matter*? 'Fraid of getting your nice clean *uniform* dirty, *superhero*?"

"No!" said Jody. "It just seems like a fool's errand to me."

"What?" said Jefferson, not understanding the metaphor.

"Even if we get out okay," Jody continued, "we'd have expended an awful lot of energy, and they'd capture us easy if we tried to fight under those circumstances. It'd just be a phyrric victory!"

"A *what*?"

"Oh, for- didn't go to any *classes* when you were at Hudson?"

"*Yes*! I *graduated, didn't* I? But they didn't teach *me* what the hell a *phallic victory* was!"

"*Phyrric*!"

"*Whatever*! What the hell does that *mean*, anyway?"

"It *means* that all the effort we would put into digging underground wouldn't be *worth* it- because we'd just get *captured* again.
"

"No, it wouldn't. Not if we do it the way I *think* we should!"

"And I suppose you're going to tell me you have *experience* digging out of places like this?"

"Darn right I do. I've escaped from more rattletrap jails than you can *count*. Have *you*?"

"A...couple times," Jody admitted. "But not *underground*."

"I've done it under. You let me do the prep work, and then you can pull your weight with all of your junk to push and shove us out of the logjams..."

"It is *not* junk!"

"*Stop* being so damn *defensive*! I wasn't trying to *insult* you! I just don't know the right term for all of your technological crap..."

"Just *stop* it!" Jody ordered. "If you don't know a *good* way to refer to my kind and my abilities, don't talk about them *at all*!"

"Well, *pardon me*!" said Jefferson, sarcastically.

She tapped the earth with a booted foot to find a spot in it where the dirt would yield to her touch. This, she explained, was the key to finding a source for a potential tunnel. Eventually, she found a yielding spot, and started using her paws to dig a hole in the ground. She was well into the task before she realized Jody had not joined her in digging. The robot seemed to be inexperienced in the process, given the awe-inspired look she seemed to have at Jefferson's enacting of it.

"You know," Jefferson said to Jody when she realized this, "this would go a *lot* quicker if you *helped* me!"

"But I...don't know how to....*do* that!" Jody admitted again.

"WHAT? You're a DOG- or at least you *look* like one. Digging is our *birthright,* girl! Didn't those government people who booted you up actually program any *real ancestral genes* in you?"

"For *fighting,* yes! But, since we're so evolved as a species now, they didn't think anything else was necessary."

"I guess you don't *hump hydrants*, either."

"You are so *vulgar*!"

Jody was still annoyed with Jefferson, but she was far less angry with her than she had been before. Anyone who could fight *her*, the most powerful robot dog in the universe, to a standstill, as Jefferson had, while perhaps not entirely worthy of respect, was, at the very least, someone who might be able to teach her some things she couldn't learn at Hudson. So, with these words, she jumped down to the hole Jefferson had made.

"What can I do to help?" Jody asked.

"You got anything inside you that can help us plot a course out of here?" Jefferson responded.

"You mean, in terms of my strength and agility, or my positronic brainwaves, or my heat rays, or my lasers, or my...?"

"Use whatever you want, kid. The important thing is that you find us a way out of here. Nothing fancy, you understand. I'm not the big brain type."

"I'm not, either. Well, if you want something simple and direct, the best thing I can think of is that I should just smash down through the Earth like a pneumatic drill and push through until we get out."

"And what will *I* be doing?"

"*You'll* be lying on my back and hanging onto my belly. Tight- if you want to stay on."

"Whoa, whoa, whoa, whoa, whoa!"

"What's *wrong* with that?"

"Isn't that....you know...?"

"That's *absurd*. We *hate* each other, don't we? You said so yourself. Besides, I'll bet you and your friend have done this kind of thing before..."

"You take that *back*!"

"Easy! I just meant that you probably hang onto each other for dear life when you need to travel quick and light. Sam does it with me all the time, and he hardly *ever* complains!"

"Why *should* he? He's a *guy*, right?"

Jefferson uttered these words with a leer that surprised Jody, as if she intended to hit on him when and if they met. So Jody shot Jefferson down in advance.

"He's *gay*!"

"*Damn* it!"

"Besides, you yourself called me a MACHINE, and MACHINES can't fall in *love*, or have *feelings*..."

"Look, I was a little *harsh* then..."

"*I'll* say you were! Look! My point *is*, you can hang onto me without people misinterpreting it as a sexual act. Especially considering *your* reputation!"

Here Jody surprised Jefferson by leering knowingly at her a la Groucho Marx, which made the latter laugh.

"You know, kid," Jefferson said as she clutched Jody's torso, "you really ain't as stuck-up as I thought you were to start with! Now, let's get out of here and kick some ass!"

"Roger Wilco!" Jody affirmed.

And so, as Jefferson held onto her for dear life, Jody jumped into the air, executed a swan dive, and, with both of her powerful legs and fists smashing away, crashed through the dirt floor of the cell and moved towards the outside world.

*

Given Jody's speed and Jefferson's "encouragement"- which took the form of kicking her boots on Jody's torso like a jockey giving similar encouragement to a racehorse- the process of drilling under the Earth proceeded smoothly. Unfortunately (or, given Jefferson's thirst for adventure, fortunately), they ended up popping out of the Earth not on the exterior of the villains' compound, as they had planned, but smack dab in the middle of it, with members of both villainous forces spotting and streaming towards them as they emerged.

As soon as they got to their feet, Jefferson and Jody knew there was only one way out of their predicament.

"We're going to have to fight them," Jody observed. "There's no other way out of this if we're going to save our friends. You up for a scrap?"

"Hell, I'm *always* up for a *scrap*!" said Jefferson. "Just let 'em at me!"

"Great!" Jody said. "Just don't get in my way, okay? We've hit each other *enough* tonight!"

"Yeah," said Jefferson. "Let's make it easy on ourselves. You take Flebus' guys, and I'll take Remus.'"

"Sure!" responded Jody. "No prob."

They fist-bumped to affirm their new loyalty to each other, and set about towards attacking their respective targets.

Jefferson's approach with taking on Remus' "men" was one that she had employed a number of times before, and she saw no reason to tamper with success. All she needed to do was simply stand stoically in the pathway of her attackers as they approached. Then, when there was very little standing between her and them, she began performing a lewd and highly lascivious cheerleading routine with the energy of at least three girls half her age. As was usually the case, the alien dogs were all sexually aroused by her performance, and, seeing each other now purely as rivals for her affections, they began to attack each other instead of her. While they killed each other, Jefferson cleared a path for herself through the smoke of battle and escaped.

Jody was not as fortunate in her battle with the alien ninja lizards. She was unable to resort to the methods Jefferson used, chiefly because of the difference in species and corporeal origin between them. Granted, she was able to hold them off for a while. Her deadly accuracy with her internal weapons, as well as her enormous, seemingly boundless physical energy, honed in many a similar battle and an equal number of athletic sporting contests, helped her keep her ground at first. And this did allow her to knock out a few of her opponents in a prime of life. But it was, ultimately, a lost cause. In addition to their other remarkable powers, the alien lizards possessed something of a hive mentality, which allowed them to assume, collectively, the form of a giant figure bigger than even Jody when they needed to. Such a figure was constructed just as Jody started to really decimate their numbers, and it proceeded to shoot a large bolt of lightning at her before she, stunned, could move out of the way- an act that significantly shocked, burned and weakened her.

Knowing that she was beaten without assistance, Jody made a mental signal to her rival-cum-comrade.

"Jefferson!" Jody "said" simply. "HELP!"

Fortunately, Jefferson had just escaped her entanglement and promptly arrived at Jody's side. Just in time, for Jody, who had been burned severely by the lightning, had large amounts of dark coal-like dust on her pelt and uniform, and had lost so much of her strength that she could barely move, let alone defend herself against the alien monster.

"He the one that hurt you?" Jefferson said, pointing at the mega-lizard. Jody nodded weakly.

"You leave him to *me*," was the response.

The monstrous lizard roared as soon as it saw Jefferson, but, she, unafraid, roared back at it.

"SHADDAP!" Jefferson said, using the same aggressive word and tone she had used earlier on Jody. That same aggression fueled a punch she threw at the beast, which promptly caused it to shatter into its dozens of components and flee in the opposite direction.

Jefferson rushed back to Jody.

"Can you keep going?" she asked. "Or are you done?"

"I...can't do...*anything* right now," Jody said. "They...hit me with...*lightning*...crossed with....*radiation*...I could *die* if I don't get a power boost soon. I was due for one, anyway."

"A power boost?"

"Yeah. That's how I get my strength and my energy. Direct hits of electricity. But, if I don't get them on a regular basis, I get too weak to fight. And, if I don't get enough after forty-eight hours, I become permanently inoperable!"

"Well, how do you *get* these power boosts? We'll *both* need to be on our game to get out of here!"

"Only my monitor can supply me with my power boosts. American Intelligence policy."

"And who's your monitor?"

"Sam."

"The same guy you're trying to...?"

"The *very* same."

"Then we *have* to find him. Can you walk?"

"Not far."

"Then I'll *carry* you."

"WHAT? You don't have to..."

"No!" Jefferson was firm in her voice, almost calcified. "I may *not* be the most *intelligent* or *refined* girl around town, but I understand when I've made a *stupid* mistake. And that was trying to *clobber* you when I should have been *working* with you to stop our enemies *together*. Yeah, I *know* that this whole thing started 'cause I was jealous of you supposedly being a better athlete than me, but, the thing is, you were right to call me out on it. I w*as* living in the past instead of the present or future, and we *both* ended up paying a price for it. Well, *not anymore*. We are *both* getting our revenge tonight, and you *are* getting that power boost you need. And *no more arguments* about it! Get me?"

"I...understand," Jody said. And she did.

X.

Meanwhile, back at the ranch....

Once Hamilton and Sam could no longer hear their friends speaking, they took their ears from the walls and looked at each other.

"That's some situation Jefferson and Jody got themselves into," said Sam. "Imagine! Getting into a big fight with each other like that- and *then* finding out somebody *filmed* the whole thing!"

"It wasn't *their* fault they go filmed," Hamilton answered. "They had no idea. What hurts me *more* is that they had to just *stand* there, in *chains*, while those....*bastards* OGLED them like that!"

"Yeah, I know," Sam answered. "It's *not* nice!"

"You sound like somebody did that to you...at one time. Or...maybe you..."

"I would never *dare* to do that!"

Hamilton smiled hearing that.

"Sam," she said, "I've been around the universe a bit, and I don't think I've *ever* heard a boy say that *once*."

"I have *standards*," he answered. "I guess that's why I haven't met anyone I could have a long-term relationship with yet."

"Except Jody."

"*She* doesn't *count*. First of all, she's a *friend*, second of all, I don't normally "do" girls, like I said before, and third, she's a *robot*. So…"

"And you never even *tried* to make love to a girl in your life?"

"When I was younger. In middle school. Just started getting it up, then, so, for some weird reason, I thought I was real cool 'cause of that. But when I tried to test out my new powers of masculinity, I got verbally burned by the girl. Bad. One of the resident athletes- a guy- saw me flame out and took pity on me. And things…kind of got…serious after that."

"I know how it is. In my first battalion, a lot of the girls were…on the other team, but I stayed clean. I was a careerist then. And, if I wanted to keep my job or get a better one higher in the ranks, I really had to play it clean. No possible tainting of my record in *any* way, if you know what I mean. They're pretty strict about those things in the military- then and now. But it's cost me as a civilian trying to establish romantic relationships. I've tried to have boyfriends over the years, but it never really worked out when I did. Hell, the longest term relationship I've ever had in my life outside of my family has been with JEFFERSON! But, fortunately for *me*, she's a clean, straight hetero when it comes to sex. Otherwise, given how big and strong she is, I'd be in *big trouble* at bedtime if we ever both decided to turn lesbian! No chance of that, though- especially not *her*."

"That kind of situation is the kind I'm always trying to avoid in a relationship. You know- big old guy wanting a rump roll with a small, sweet innocent young thing. I see myself more in the latter category, by the way, given my age and the fact that a lot of the guys I have an interest in are older and/or bigger than me. But I don't advertise myself or my abilities publically, like those pissy drag queens do. In my "tribe", we generally tend to hide our light under a bushel until it's magic time. Because you really have to be careful, given how people are out to get us all the time. I had to wait until high school and I became a cheerleader to even *think* about publicly flirting with a guy- the girls on the team gave me a lot of pointers there. It's really a lot easier giving with the goo-goo eyes and the wolf whistles and the come-hither purring than it is for me to actually *do* it with a guy, you know."

"You don't *seem* that limp-wristed to *me*. Maybe an *experienced* girl like me could help you start feeling like a hetero again."

"You're starting to *flirt* with me again, aren't you, Major?"

"Please! Call me *Hamilton! You* haven't insisted on me calling you "Agent Poodle", *have* you?"

"No. But respect demands that I..."

"*Fuck* respect! More to the point- fuck *ME*!"

She put her paw underneath his sweater, he put his underneath her shirt, and soon they were undressing each other...

*

Despite the added weight of Jody Ryder in her arms, Jefferson Ball was still able to run at a formidable speed. She had to- for, once again, the heroines had been discovered by their enemies, and needed to make a quick getaway to avoid annihilation.

As a consequence, Jefferson was running deftly, managing to avoid at all costs the various lasers, bullets and bolts of lightning being aimed at her. Likewise, she was taking great pains not to expose Jody to further damage when she was clearly not in a position to be able to save herself. The robot knew this, and decided to voice her feelings at this moment.

"Jefferson?" she said.

"What?" was the answer.

"I'm sorry. I never should have called you a drunken has-been, because obviously you *aren't*. I mean, going to all this trouble to *save* me..."

"It's accepted," Jefferson grunted. "I apologized already, so it's good you're doing it, too."

"I wouldn't be a hero if I didn't admit I was wrong and made a mistake. That's how it seems to go, doesn't it?"

"Darn right it does. But why are you even still talking if you're partway to being broken down? I would've thought..."

"My vocal apparatus is separate from the rest of my body. It can only be destroyed along with the rest of me if I decide to self-destruct to take somebody out. Especially if it's *me*."

"You don't feel that way now, do you?"

"No! Why are you asking?"

"Because our "pals" back there have just thrown a *bomb* in our direction! And it looks like it's going to take the *both* of us out, vocal cords and all!"

"WHAT?"

Yet, before anything could be done, the bomb landed right on the path in front of them, forcing Jefferson to come to a complete stop. And then it exploded, throwing Jefferson and Jody into the air, screaming....

XI.

Hamilton Pomeranian was lying on the floor, naked save for her dashiki and underclothes, an expression of satisfaction on her face. As would be expected from someone who had been "done" with precision by someone who, though inexperienced, clearly had known what needed to be done. But her partner, as much as he had enjoyed the experience, was now, half-dressed, with his skirt now back around his waist, was showing pains of regret over what he had done. Or *might* have done.

Sam Poodle was staring out the bars of the cell, looking to see if anyone had seen or heard what he and Hamilton had done just now. He worried chiefly about the consequences for Hamilton, but also nagging at his back was his own sexual status. Namely- how could he consider himself "gay" now that he had "done" it with a *girl*?

While he was thinking this, Hamilton, having donned her pants, came over to Sam and put her paw on his bottom. He immediately withdrew.

"What is it, Sam?" she asked. "I hope I didn't..."

"No," Sam replied. "But I think I *did*."

"How could you have done *that*? I was *enjoying* myself..."

"Now. But in a few months..."

"The hell are you *talking* about?"

"You're a girl, and I'm a boy, and we did it, and naturally..."

"*Not* naturally. I'm sterile."

"*Guh*?"

Sam was stunned, as he had become accustomed to being around Hamilton.

"The accident that destroyed my eye and my leg also fried my eggs," Hamilton said. "Consequently, if someone like you tries to disadvantage me like you did, there are no consequences for me reproduction-wise. So I can take it good whenever a guy lays his jackhammer on me and enjoy it, just like with you just now. I think that's one of the reasons Jeff likes me so much. She can take just as much as I can, if not more. And *she* isn't even *sterile*."

"Bully for you on *that*," Sam said. "But what about *me*?"

"What *about* you?"

"How can I call myself *gay* now that I've *done it* with a *girl*?"

"Simple. Don't tell anyone this happened. *I'm* not gonna. It can be our little secret. You can go back to being gay, and I..."

"Thanks. But my psyche is kind of delicate, and I don't know if..."

"Oh, for...Don't you know any guys who are *bi*?"

"Buy *what*?"

"*Bisexual*!"

"What does *that* mean?"

Hamilton was surprised at Sam's naivete for a moment, but then she remembered that he *was* just a high school student, and wasn't yet exposed to *all* of the sexual activities of the world. So she spoke again to him, after a moment, as if instructing a child- clearly and directly.

"It *means* that you sleep with both *boys* and *girls*- sometimes together, sometimes separately."

"You can *do* that?"

"Uh...*Yeah*! If you *want* to. But you get a lot of flack for it if you do. More than you would if you were just gay, but them's the conditions that prevail, son."

"It can't be any worse than just being gay. It's not exactly a *picnic* being *that*."

"I gathered that. But the good thing about it is, if you ever get tired of chasing boys, you can chase *girls* instead. Like *me*, for instance!"

She seemed to be eager to pull him down to the floor for another jackhammer session, and he was not exactly refusing her. But that would have to wait. An enormous crash struck the building, and both of them were thrown about the cell by the impact.

"What the hell was *that*?" said Sam.

"I don't know," responded Hamilton. "But we better look presentable for whoever it is- if it *is* a someone. Put your sweater on and hand me my shirt."

He hastened to follow her instructions.

*

The crash, of course, was the result of Jefferson and Jody crashing into the jail building where Hamilton and Sam were being held as a result of the ricochet from the exploding bomb. They had no idea that their friends were there, but, once they landed- in the exterior of the cells rather than inside of one, fortunately- they had a clear hunch that this was the place they needed to be to find them.

"Come on!" Jefferson said, once they had recovered from the crash's impact. "They're *bound* to be in one of these cells. Are you still okay with your operations? We might need your x-ray eyes, 'cause I can't see through wood..."

"Oh, my senses are all right," responded Jody. "I just picked up Sam's scent. I'd recognize his body odor *anywhere*- even if I *wasn't* a robot!"

"Then, for pity's sake, let's go g*et* them!"

They only had to trot a short distance, fortunately for Jody's much reduced powers of endurance. These circumstances were also why it was Jefferson, rather than Jody, who proceeded, with a mighty kick, to knock the door of the cell off of its hinges. It was made of a much weaker material than the door of the cell Jefferson and Jody had been imprisoned in, obviously. Hamilton and Sam, initially fearful, backed away in the corner- until they saw their friends enter. This was cause for a short, passionate, if muted, reunion between them.

"What the *hell*?" said Hamilton. "You two are *pals* now?"

She had clearly noticed the absence of enmity between the pair, as had Sam, and was particularly shocked that Jefferson in particular no longer saw Jody as her archenemy. They were quick to explain themselves.

"Jody here and I came to an understanding," said Jefferson. "*She's* the strongest *robot* in the universe, and *I'm* the greatest *meatbag* adventuress in it. And anyone who thinks *otherwise* is gonna have to deal with us *both*!"

"Besides," Jody added solemnly. "What we went through at the hands of those *cheap bump 'n' grind merchants* is enough to make *any* two people friends. Even if they were *enemies* to *start* with!"

"We know," Hamilton said, pointing to the wall. "We heard the whole sordid affair. Damn things are like *paper*."

"So the offices are next door?" Jefferson asked.

"Should be," said Sam, "if we heard everything they said!"

"Then we should go next door and deck *all* of them!" Jefferson said.

"I'm all for that," Jody said. "What about you two?"

Hamilton and Sam nodded.

"Okay," the robot responded. "But first, I need a power boost. You have your stuff, Sam?"

"Sure do," Sam said, unzipping a pocket sewed into his skirt. "Wouldn't *think* of leaving it behind, J.R. And- if I may say- you really look like you *need* one this time!"

"I *did* get struck by lightning," Jody said, though without malice. She knew him too well to be offended by the comment.

As Jefferson and Hamilton watched, Jody opened a compartment in her arm, and Sam, withdrawing a miniature set of jumper cables, stuck the outlets into sockets in the compartment Jody had exposed. Then, flicking a switch on a portable control unit also contained in the pocket, Sam sent a much needed surge of electricity flowing into Jody's body. There was a flash of smoke and heat, and Jody screamed at first when the electricity hit her, but her scream soon modulated into an ululation of empowerment, even pleasure. When it was over, Jody- with all the dusty grime tainting her pelt and uniform now magically gone- flexed her renewed arm muscles, and grinned at Sam with an affectionate smile that also reflected this renewed wattage. He sent this knowing grin back to her as he removed the equipment from her arm and put it back in his pocket as she closed the compartment.

"Thanks, Sam!" Jody said. "I *needed* that! Now I'm ready to *fight* again, Jefferson!"

"And I'll fight *with* you this time, Jody!" Jefferson replied. "Come on!"

The pair rushed out, only to be halted by a cry of "Hold it!" coming from both Hamilton and Sam. This sent them back in.

"*What*?" Jefferson and Jody asked together.

"You're just going to go in *cold*?" Hamilton said.

"With no *plan*?" added Sam.

"You guys heard what they *did* to us, *didn't you*?" asked Jefferson. "*Revenge* is our plan!"

"*Revenge* is gonna get you *killed*!" observed Hamilton. "*And*, let me remind you *both*, that it was *revenge* that got you- not to *mention* me and Sam- into this predicament to *start* with!"

"So?" asked Jody.

"*So*," said Sam, "we can't just go in there and take names! Remus and Flebus have their retinues with them all the time, so they *outnumber* us! *And*, even *if* we were to somehow even the score, we couldn't take the edge with a direct assault. Hell- *one* of us might survive," – here he pointed at Jody- "but *three* of us would have at least *one* cap shot up our asses when it was all finished!"

"That's tellin' 'em, Sam!" Hamilton said, holding his paw affectionately.

Inadvertently, she had given away their relationship, causing Jefferson and Jody to both gasp in horrified shock. The latter put her paws over her mouth, while the former clutched a paw to her formidable breasts. Hamilton, realizing what she had done, separated from Sam quickly. But the damage, as such, had been done.

"*What*?" said Sam, who didn't feel as much as Hamilton the need to disguise their relationship. "It's not like we did anything *wrong* by making *love* to each other, *is it*?"

"You mean," Jody said, taking her paws off of her mouth, "you actually..."

"Yes!" said a frustrated Hamilton. "But Sam's *right*. Love making's not a *crime*! If it *was*," –she pointed to Jefferson at this point- "then *you'd* be on DEATH ROW!"

"Ha, ha!" retorted Jefferson sarcastically. Then, to Jody, she said: "I *thought* you said he was *gay*!"

"He *is*!" Jody answered. "Unless he's been *hiding* it from me *all this time*!" She glared suspiciously at him at this point.

"*Why* in the *world* would I *fake* something that's *totally* who I *am?*" Sam responded to Jody. Lowering his tone, and with a tinge of regret on his part, he added: "At least, something I *thought* was a part of who I am."

"You have *nothing* to be ashamed of, Sam," Hamilton said, in his defense and her own indictment. "It was *totally my fault*. Both of us didn't know when the hell we were getting out of this rathskellar- if at *all*- it was confining and hot in here, and we had nothing *better* to do! Besides, I was totally in *love* with him from the first time I set eyes on him!"

"You think *I wasn't?*" Sam said as they held paws again. "Hamilton, you could charm the skin off a *snake* if you wanted to!"

"Look who's talking, charm magnet!" she answered.

"But why didn't you *tell* us you were doing the big nasty together?" Jefferson interjected. "It would have saved us a lot of aggravation to *know, Hamilton,* that you'd gone to all the trouble of starting to *convert* gay guys..."

"*Because* we were restricted to the confining environment of this perfectly *idyllic* and *luxurious* strip of *concrete* with very little *hope* of *escape*, you pompous, thick headed ASSHOLE!" Hamilton shouted, as she and Sam advanced on Jefferson, angrily. "How in the *hell* were we supposed to *contact* you? They *stole* our cell phones, and there isn't even a goddamn *socket* in here. Let alone a wi-fi hotspot!"

"And she did *not* "convert" me, you prejudiced PRICK!" added Sam. "She just made me realize that I could make myself available to *girls* as well as *boys*- and still be able to take some *pride* in what I am!"

"As *if* there's any way *you* could have *pride* in being a stupid PANSY!" snapped a short tempered Jefferson to Sam, revealing her prejudices in this matter. "And *you*," she added, turning to her friend, "should know *better* than to *turn tricks* after telling me *not* to all the time!"

"I was *not "turning TRICKS"!*" blazed Hamilton. "You should know me *better* than that!"

"And you don't even *know* me!" protested Sam. "You can't *judge* me just because I'm..."

"Both of you BACK OFF if you *don't* want *fat lips*!" responded Jefferson.

They didn't.

They argued fiercely and hotly for several minutes, with almost the same intensity with which Jefferson had physically fought Jody earlier in the evening. The robot initially was merely a spectator, fascinated at how an organic being's sexuality- a topic that, truth be said, held as much interest to her as a university course would have to an elementary school student- could be a topic of such passionate debate. Eventually, though, annoyed at the time and opportunity being squandered by the others, she interjected herself into the debate with a sound from her internal audio archives- the roar of the MGM lion. That got the attention of the others quickly.

"I find this whole line of inquiry *fascinating*," Jody muttered sarcastically. "But it's also entirely *irrelevant*! *Everyone* should be allowed to choose *whatever* sexual vocation they *want*- and to be entirely *free* of the kind of *malicious* debate the three of you are engaging in regarding it!"

"And I supposed that means I can't *object* to these things if I want to?" asked Jefferson.

"You can," Jody said, "so long as you do *nothing* to prevent them from happening!"

"Try to do *nothing* to stop my *fist* from *hitting you, metal mouth*!" Jefferson snapped. Hamilton and Sam blocked their respective friends from becoming violent with each other again.

"Look, Jenny..." Hamilton began.

"JODY!" the robot thundered.

"Sorry- Jody," the ex-soldier corrected herself with genuine apologetic feelings. "This has just been a *long* night. For *all* of us. And all the *negative* things we've said about each other tonight we know from *experience* with each other are *not true*. And we'll all *regret* saying them- either now or later."

As Hamilton and Sam backed away from Jefferson and Jody, they embraced on friendly terms. Then Jefferson beckoned Hamilton and Sam forward again.

"Look," she said. "You *both* have a point. The thing is, Sam, that you're right. I *don't* know you- yet. And, to be honest, most of the experiences I've had with your kind of fellow in the past have been- well, let's say, not the most *pleasant* of experiences. And, in general, I'm not exactly *kind* to folks who *are* or who *might* be like that 'cause of that. Anyway, I'm sorry I made such a bad impression on you just now, and, if you and Hammy are *serious* about this, I'll support *both* of you. Hamilton, I'm sorry, too. I *do* know you better than that, and I only said that 'cause the stress started getting to me. Just 'cause you roll around once or twice doesn't make you a slut. It's a lot of other things that have mostly happened to *me*, not you. And, Jody, we already apologized to each other *once* tonight, so we don't need to do it again, do we?"

"No, Jefferson", Jody said. "I know. And I'm proud of you for being able to eat crow like that so quickly. But all of this doesn't *begin* to resolve our central *problem* here. Which is: how do we get our revenge on Remus, Flebus and their forces for hurting us- *all* of us- destroy that rotten film before they can exhibit it, and- most importantly- get *out* of here with a shred of our collective *dignity* left?"

"This is where Sam and I can make ourselves useful to *you* instead of each other, as has been the case of late," remarked Hamilton. "I got battle plans in my head I haven't even *used* yet."

"Yeah," said Sam. "And Jody and I still have a few unused things in our *own* playbook."

"Well, let's discuss what to *do*, already," interjected Jefferson. "With all your stuff, we ought to come up with *something.*"

The four of them came together in a football huddle, talking quietly- for once- so their scheme would not be overheard.

XII.

"ESCAPED? What the hell do you *mean*, "escaped"? That stupid door was supposed to be IMPENETRABLE!"

Remus The Twenty Third had just been informed, by two of his soldiers, of the fact that Jefferson Ball and Jody Ryder were out of their cells. Not only that, but Sam Poodle and Hamilton Pomeranian were also gone- presumably freed by their friends. This was not a good turn of events for the monarchs, and Remus showed it in the rage that now creased its face. Flebus, on the other hand, was calm, almost placid- or so it seemed.

"The door was untouched, sir," said one of the reporting soldiers. "But there was a big hole in the middle..."

"BLAST IT!" Remus shot up from his chair in uncontained fury. "That *maniac DUG* her way out! *And* she convinced that robotic *louse* to along *with* her!"

"You shouldn't characterize Jody Ryder as a "louse"," interjected Flebus, calmly. "I myself can think of many *worse* things than *that* to call her!"

"And why the hell are *you* so calm?" Remus shot at his fellow monarch. "This is as much *your* problem as it is *mine!*"

"Because *you're* just going to solve the problem *yourself*- like you *always* do," Flebus countered, revealing the steel behind his chilly exterior. "Me and my boys haven't had much to *do* with the lot of *you* around!"

"And *what*, exactly, does *that* mean?" said Remus, angrily.

"It *means* that, as far as this enterprise has been going, I have become merely a *minority shareholder-* rather than the *equal partner* I *should* be!"

"How do you figure *that*? I've consulted with you all the way on *everything...*"

"...and then gone ahead and done whatever the hell you want!"

"We're splitting distribution on the stag reel..."

"...and *I* get the less *populated* areas of the universe, so I get less *money* from the deal!"

"*And* I made sure that you would be treated with the same respect as *I* am..."

"Just like the *tramps* and *charlatans* and other *con men* in your so-called "court"."

"Honest to God! How can you say that after all I've *done* for you?"

" 'All' you've done for me! Name *one* thing you've "done" for me since we hooked up!"

"I made sure your worthless GOLDBRICKS worked alongside my *supreme examples of canine masculinity* on this gig, *didn't I?* If I wasn't such a democratic fellow, they would've stayed behind- just like *you* should have!"

"What the hell do you mean by *that*, you...?"

"What I mean to *say*, FLEAB, is that I'm starting to have *serious doubts* about us continuing to work together like this! Now that the girls are *out-* which I blame YOU for, FLEAB, by the way- our jig will likely be UP soon! Isn't that right, FLEAB?"

"No, REAM- which is what I want to *do* to you right now- it's *not*! If you weren't such a pig headed *egotist* who needs to have his own way *all the time*, REAM, we might actually have *trapped* the *ladies* once and for all like we *planned*! Ain't that the solid truth, REAM baby?"

"DO *NOT* ADDRESS ME IN THOSE *FAMILIAR* TONES, YOU INSIGNIFICANT SPECK OF DUST! *I* am REMUS THE TWENTY THIRD, heir to the *Pine Top Throne* and undisputed *ruler* of my planet- not to mention the *six* planets *nearest yours*- AND I WILL BE ADDRESSED WITH *RESPECT*- by *you* and EVERYONE ELSE!"

"I do not *need* to address *you* with *respect* when I can *kill* you just by *touching* you! And I am the Grand Master of *all* Ninja Lizards! If I cannot do it alone, then I can easily call my forces to do the same!"

"You *think* so? Let's see if they can do that when *my* boys fill 'em full of BUCKSHOT! And *you*, too- if you're not careful!"

"Your bullets do not scare me- and neither do your *words*!"

They glared at each other, silently, for a moment. Then, Remus noticed that the two soldiers he had spoken to earlier were still standing at attention.

"What the hell are *you* still here for?" he snarled. "Get your asses in gear and *find* those two *B cups* before they try anything funny! That goes for the rest of you boys, too! And you lazy lizard fellows, besides! Earn your damn *keep*, will you?"

Remus then glared at Flebus and received an angry glare in return. They then turned heel and walked off in opposite directions, like a married couple about to permanently separate. Which, in a sense, they already were.

*

Seconds after they separated, the doorbell rang, and Remus, seeing as everyone else seemed to be *occupied* doing one thing or another, went to the door of the lavish hideout. When he opened the door, he found a small Pomeranian there, making with the big eyes as she stood there in her underclothes. This, of course, was Hamilton, but, as she had disfigured her pristine facial features with a liberal application of wet dirt, she hoped the dog king wouldn't recognize her. And well he might. She had shot him with her personal firearm in his privates in a previous encounter, and he still boasted to all in hearing range that he would strangle her to death for that if they ever met again. But, since they'd had no face to face time yet in this adventure, there was still the chance that this might happen. Hence this subterfuge.

The *reason* why Hamilton was standing there, scraggly furred and underdressed, was an outgrowth of the plan she, Jefferson, Jody and Sam had devised only moments earlier. Hamilton, as already noted, was the only one of the group whom Remus had neither seen nor spoken too during the course of events of this story. Consequently, she was the best bet of the four to "con" her way into the building, and allow the others to enter secretly from the roof- to launch a surprise attack. The original plan was for Hamilton to play a Pup Scout, since she resembled the puppies of some larger breeds, although she was an adult Pomeranian, perceivably selling cookies door to door. However, that plan was abandoned because they didn't have a proper uniform, and Jody could only produce costume changes for her own body. So they decided, instead, that Hamilton would pose as a member of Remus' army, who had been robbed on her way to base and needed assistance. It wasn't the best idea any of them could think of on such short notice, but it would have to do given their desperate circumstances. Hamilton initially objected to the idea of running around in her underwear, fearful as she was of being taunted for it (or worse)- until Jefferson reminded her that *she* did it all the time, and *she* didn't get taunted all the time for it, *did* she?

That shut Hamilton up.

So there Hamilton stood, deposited there by Jody Ryder (who had also impersonated the doorbell through her sound effects library) before she rejoined the others on the roof. Remus looked at her suspiciously.

"What the hell do *you* want?" he demanded.

"Oh, mighty king!" Hamilton said as she bowed down in front of him, in the vastly exaggerated tones of a medieval vassal. "I am but a humble soldier in your forces who has lost her way in the woods- and, in the process, was robbed of my raiment and my meager possessions by villains skilled in banditry! I humbly seek shelter in your..."

"Yeah, yeah, yeah!" Remus interrupted, curtly. "I *get* it! Listen, uh...."

"Major Falstaff Oppenshaw," Hamilton said, saluting. "Of the Fred Allen Battalion Of The 52nd Remulan Infantry..."

"All *right,* already! Get in here, slap on a toga, wash your smelly face, and report for duty!"

"Blessings upon you, sire. I...."

"Cut that *out*! I get enough glad-handing around here as it is. I don't need *any more* right now!"

He ushered her inside with a wave of his paw, and she ran inside. He didn't notice her chirping that she was "in" into a portable wrist communicator (Sam's- which he had loaned her for the purpose of the con) as she did.

"She seems like a good kid," Remus observed as he closed the door.

Then, suddenly, he realized a few things.

"*Wait* a *minute*! My armed forces are all *guys*. No dames allowed. And since *when* do we have a doorb..."

He spotted Hamilton running down a hallway and pointed at her.

"Hey, *you*! BITCH! Get BACK here!"

She didn't. She ran. He pursued her.

Although she was fast- and had the 100m dash rushing trophies at home to prove it- he was no slouch, either, and soon he was catching up to her.

"HELP!" Hamilton bellowed into the communicator.

But it seemed like her friends wouldn't be able to help her this time. Especially when one of Remus' soldiers came to block the doorway in front of her, startling her enough to allow for the dog king to grab her by the arm and pull her back towards him from behind. He wiped the dirt from Hamilton's face with one paw, revealing her true identity, while holding her tightly with the other. Through this process, he came to recognize her.

"Well," he said, snidely. "If it isn't *you*. My *crotch* hasn't been the same since you put a *bullet* in it. For a while there, I was practically pissing LEAD!"

He laughed viciously, as did the soldiers who now came to surround him, as he threw Hamilton violently to the ground.

"Hamilton, isn't it?" he asked her rhetorically, with contempt. "*Major* Hamilton Pomeranian? Of the Star Soldiers?"

"Right," she answered, in a defiant tone. "Retired. But no *less* threatening in spite of *that*!"

"Oh, *come on*!" answered Remus. "I can understand you speaking to me like that if you had actually had the *nerve* to pull a *gun* on me- like you did *last* time we met! But, the way you're dressed right *now*, I *hardly* think you've even got enough space to *conceal* one on your person. And, as you can see for yourself, you're pretty well outnumbered here. If, somehow, you were to get away from *me*, I can just have one of the boys here put a bullet in your back as soon as he spots you making a dash for our egress. *That'll* be the end of you for *sure*. So what gives with the *chutzpah*?"

"I...don't know," said Hamilton, suddenly unsure of herself. (What was *keeping* the *others*?) "Old habits, I guess."

"Well, I don't know what to do with you," Remus observed brusquely. "I got *enough* girls in my harem on Remula *as it is*. The best thing I can *think* of, given how you *duped* me so badly like that, is just turn you over to Flebus and have him put you out of your misery with his "magic" fingers. You know he's got enough electricity in his body to kill you *stone dead* if he even *touches* you, right? Not at all like that penny ante shanghai bit his boys gave you earlier. Trouble is, he's gone all *Diva* on me now, so we're gonna have to *sneak* you into his clutches..."

"Don't you call *me* a *Diva, Remus! You're the biggest motherfucking DIVA in the UNIVERSE!*"

Flebus was now there, along with the closest members of his retinue. He pushed his way forwards towards Remus and over Hamilton, who was careful to avoid his touch.

"Listen, guys," Hamilton said. "I should really be..."

"SHUT UP!" Remus and Flebus said at the same time. The former brought her to her feet and held her in place with a powerful arm. With the other one, he withdrew his branding iron.

"*I'm* killing her!" Remus said, suddenly possessive now that Flebus was actually there, instead of just being absent. "Soon as I put my *brand* on her, she's *mine!*"

"Please!" Flebus said, dismissively. "You put your "brand" on *Jefferson Ball* earlier in the night, and *that* didn't make her "yours" by *any* means."

"*That* was *different*! I was just showing *her* who was the *boss* around here!"

"With the *delightful* result being that she's *escaped*- and is no doubt seeking to avenge herself on *both* of us! Not to *mention* that she has that robotic dimbulb Jody Ryder on her *side* now- though I *doubt* that you putting that *bucket* on her *head* made *her* think any more *highly* of you than *Jefferson* does!"

"Try to *stop* me, you...*reptile!*"

"I'd be *delighted* to!"

He rushed forward towards Remus, just as Remus lit his branding iron with a match, and sent it towards Hamilton's navel....

*

This Cecil B. De Mille-like tableau was, however, swiftly interrupted. Jefferson Ball snuck up from behind on Remus, tugged fiercely on his cape, and brought him flying down backwards in the most un-imperial fashion on his royal ass. Hamilton went flying, but Jefferson swiftly caught her after she had upended Remus, produced her clothing, and admonished her good naturedly to go get dressed. Which she did, after a quick jet away from the scene, and then returned in record time. Jody Ryder, meanwhile, threw her own powerful body into the path of Flebus' outstretched one. She countered the stemming electricity in his fingertips by producing a blast of same from her eyes, sending him flying backwards into the closest wall. Sam Poodle, meanwhile, snatched Remus' branding iron when it flew out of the monarch's paw, and adopted it as his own weapon for the potential fight that seemed to be brewing.

Remus, furiously angry at both the interruption and at being foiled in his aims, attempted to get to his feet, but Jefferson covered him like a professional wrestler (which she sometimes was when she *really* needed money) before he could do so.

"I've been waiting *all night* to get at *you, pal*!" she snarled, and advanced on him.

"Uh....guys?" Remus mewed weakly to his soldiers. "A little *help* here!" Then, in more appropriate tones, he added: "Your *king commands* it!"

Just after he said this, however, Jefferson Ball's paws closed around his throat.

"The *only* reason I'm *not* going to *kill* you for what you *did* to me and Jody tonight," she said, "is that it wouldn't be *fair-* or even *canine*! It's pretty ironic I had to learn that from a *robot*..."

She and Jody winked at each other here.

"...but there you go. Anyway, she's more of a *dog* than you'll *ever* be! But that's enough talk from me for tonight. Time for you to get *crowned* again, *KING*!"

She kneed him in the balls, and then stretched all of his limbs as far back as they could go, until the bones audibly cracked and he shouted out loud in pain. Then, when Jefferson was convinced he had suffered enough at her paws, she simply picked him up and threw him away, over her head, like a discarded banana peel. Upon Remus' landing on his ass- again- Sam covered him with the branding iron, intent on exacting his own revenge on the dog king.

"Give that *back*!" Remus shouted when he saw Sam holding the iron.

"I *will, honey*!" Sam leered, in the most stereotypically "gay" tone of voice he could manage, a clear cheap shot at Remus for using that exact same tone on *him* when they first met. "But *first*, let me put my *brand* on you!"

"I don't like the sound of that," Remus said, to no one in particular.

"*You* aren't *supposed* to!" Sam growled, in his normal, if enraged, tone of voice.

Ripping three matches from the supply handily available on Remus' garter belt, Sam symbolically lit each of them in turn for each time he proceeded to brand Remus with his own iron.

"*This* is for what you did to Jody and Jefferson!" he said as he branded Remus' ear.

"*This* is for what you did to me and Hamilton!" he said as he branded Remus' forehead.

"and THIS," he said, with finality, as he branded Remus' genitals, "is for calling me a FAGGOT!!!"

Remus had screamed his way through the branding process, and, with this final, blistering attack on his very doghood, he collapsed into unconsciousness. His soldiers were galvanized by this brazen attack on their king's person, but Sam held them back by aggressively brandishing the branding iron at them.

"Any of you guys want me to roast *your* chestnuts?" he said.

The soldiers nodded "no", as one.

"Then GET LOST!"

They got lost, again as one.

Jefferson and a now-dressed Hamilton approached him with affection.

"*Now* do you see why I fell in *love* with him?" Hamilton asked Jefferson.

"Actually," Jefferson admitted, "yeah!"

Jody Ryder, meanwhile, had set her sights on Flebus, who had just recovered from the blow of electricity she had given him, and was trying to make his escape undetected, along with his associates.

Too late.

"I *saw* you!" she shouted.

In seconds, she had shot across the room, and, arms crossed, firmly blocked Flebus' path.

"And where do you think *you're* going?" she asked, rhetorically.

He attempted to speak, but she had been through too much that night, as a close look at her sleep-deprived eyes came to reveal to him, to allow her to tolerate anything more in the way of insolent protest from him. Her angry glare alone tore him to ribbons. So Flebus' attempt to speak was a colossal fiasco. He stammered briefly, then fell silent.

"Flebus," she said, in the tones of the teenager she was, in particular the angered kind confronting a wrongdoing elder, "I'm ashamed of you. Completely and utterly *ashamed*. It's *bad enough* you think so highly of yourself that you think you can conquer the universe alone! No! You *also* had the unmitigated *gall* to think you could team up with that cape wearing *lunatic*- pardon me, "*KING*"- Remus, flim flam both me and Jefferson, have us practically fight each other to the *death*, *film* it, and then believe that, *somehow*, people would be willing to pay the *arm* and the *leg* you were going to *charge* them to *see* us knock each other's BLOCK off! Not to *mention* the fact that you *kidnapped* our *best friends* in order to *incite* us to the level of *primitive savagery* you *somehow* believed would make the whole goddamn thing more AUTHENTIC! And that doesn't even *begin* to include the fact that Jefferson and I had to just *sit* there while you *morons* went and treated us and our filmic doppelgangers with all the *respect* you would give

STRIPPERS in a BURLESQUE HOUSE! Even when Remus had that goddamned *bucket* put over my *head, for your information*, I still *heard* and *felt* everything without having to *see* it! The *only* reason, *sir,* that you and your associates are not *pushing up daisies* THIS MINUTE is the *same* reason Jefferson didn't kill *Remus* just now. We may take ourselves and our jobs seriously- a little *too* seriously, perhaps- but we *also* know we couldn't call ourselves *heroes* if we *weren't* able to show ourselves capable of *compassion*. Even for our erstwhile ENEMIES!"

Jody turned to Jefferson, smiling and giving a "thumbs up" gesture with her paw, which Jefferson responded to in kind. Then Jody returned to glaring at Flebus.

"The prosecution *rests*, your honor. Is the *defense* prepared to state its case?"

"I...don't have one," Flebus said, humbly. "You recapitulated all of my actions, as you always seem to *do* when we fight, and I just *can't* provide any way of justifying my actions. Please spare me and my people. Never mind that *cur*, Remus. He already *got* what was *due* him. I was merely *duped* by him and his *lies*. You *have* to believe me. I'll...I'll do *anything* you want!"

"*Anything*?" Jody raised an eyebrow with bemused suspicion.

"Anything," repeated Flebus.

"All right!" Jody said, after rolling her eyes and sighing. "Come on, you!"

She grabbed one of his ears, and pulled him down the corridor, like a teacher escorting a recalcitrant student to the principal's office. Once Jody was near Jefferson, she dropped him-harshly- in front of her.

"Jef'son!" Jody said, in the coy, innocent schoolgirl voice she had heard Jefferson using on her earlier. "Kin I *talk* to ya fer a moment?"

"Yah! Sure!" Jefferson said, recognizing and playing along with Jody's "joke", and boxing off Flebus by standing in front of him opposite Jody. "What'cha *want*, Jody?"

"I was jes *talkin'* with ol' *Fleab*, here," said Jody, "an' it *seems* like he's *willin'* ta do what-*evah* it is we *want-a* him!"

"Ya *mean* he wants ta...?" asked Jefferson, innocently.

"*Naw, silly*! I mean like Treaty 'a' Versailles-type stuff. Spoil 'a' war an' evry'thin'!"

"Uh-huh! *Dis* I likes *hearin'*!"

"An' I just *thought,* ya know, that ya might wanna *help* me figure out what it 'tis we *want* from him- reparation' wise, dat is! We was *in* this ta-*getha,* afta all!"

"Oh! Dat's *ea-sy.* Foist, an' most *importan',* thing is that he trashes *all* da copies of dat *awful stag reel* he made-a us, so dat it *never gets seen a-gin*!"

"Right, right, right, right, *right*! Say, Fleab, what type-a *stock* was that *film*-a yours *printed* on?"

"Nitrate," said Flebus.

"Well! *Den* ya can *burn* all those suckas, *ea-sy*!" preened Jefferson, giggling.

"*Right*," agreed Jody, in the same tones. "Ya got *matches* on ya, *don't* ya, Fleab?"

Flebus nodded.

"Den *dat's* done wit'" said Jody. "Second thing *is*- ya round up *all* yer folk' and get outta here as soon as ya *can*. Make sure ya wake up *Ream*, too, so dat *he* knows it, likewise. And maybe tear down dis *playhouse*-a yours, while ye're *at* it, before ya go. Dat all okay wit' *you,* Jefferson?"

"Aw! I could'na say-ed it better *myself,* Jody!" Jefferson said, continuing her mock preen. "Yer a natchal' barn *wonda*!"

"Cut out *dat* kinda *tawk*, dearie!" Jody said, in a campy tone. "Yer *embarassin'* me!"

Having concluded their elaborate impersonation of two working class New York City department store shop girls circa 1930, Jefferson and Jody briefly looked seriously down at Flebus to see if he had gotten the message beneath the joke (which he clearly had), and then across at each other again. But, in spite of their attempts to suppress the giggles that had been building up in their throats over the course of the routine, they failed in this one endeavor. Soon, they had collapsed, with raucous, unrestrained feminine laughter, into each other's arms for support. Flebus, sensing a momentary opportunity for escape, tried to crawl away from their embrace between their legs, but Jody, still on the ball in spite of her momentary hysterics, tripped him with her foot, preventing any such escape from occurring.

Iris out.

XIII.

Fade in.

A couple of days later.

News of the fact that Jefferson and Jody had jointly foiled yet another attempted invasion of Earth quickly spread, and both were quickly feted in the manner they had both become accustomed to in their heroic careers. They basked in the glow together, proud to affirm their new friendship in front of a public audience. Sam and Hamilton, however, fearful of attracting negative attention from gossip minded newsmagazines, blogs, and other scurrilous, disreputable print, film, TV and web news providers, were careful to hide their love directly from the prying eyes of the press, though sundry accusations were made in private regardless.

Following a raucous public celebration of their achievements, during which Jefferson, Hamilton and even the usually mild-mannered Sam got roaring drunk, and Jody, forgetting herself, had a little bit too much more motor oil than usual, the four of them managed to stagger to Jefferson and Hamilton's apartment house without being run over by any cars. This was because Jefferson had something "personal" she wanted to give to Jody and Sam as a way of making amends for being such an "asshole" when they first met. Hamilton well knew what that "gift" might be, given her extensive past experience with Jefferson, and she excused herself from the impending "ceremony", advising Jody and Sam to be "careful" as she slipped upstairs to her now ninja lizard free room.

As the three of them had their faculties impaired, it was sometime before they could figure out how to open Jefferson's locked apartment door, as she had, in the course of the evening's events, forgotten her keys to it. Eventually, Jody just blasted a hole through it with her internal firearm mechanism, and they were able to enter through the hole. Jefferson went into her bedroom for a moment, and then returned to Jody and Sam, bearing vestments.

"Here," Jefferson said, as she handed two of the many of the copies of her trademark outfit she owned to Jody and Sam, who seemed genuinely surprised to get them. "Consider this a peace offering, if we haven't made peace already. This way, if we don't actually cross paths again- although I hope we *do*, under more *friendly* conditions- you'd remember me in a *good* way, instead of for being such a low-balling *jerk*, like I was to start with."

"Oh, Jefferson," Jody said, getting artificially teary-eyed. "That's such a lovely, unselfish gesture on your part. Especially since *I* was as much of a jerk as *you* were in the course of the whole thing." Then, slightly more soberly, she added: "Still, I couldn't actually *wear* this. I don't want any one seeing the *disaster area* my *belly* is. Besides, this is *your* look. I could no more ask you to wear one of *my* suits than you asking me to..."

"I'm not saying you should be *wearing* it, kid," Jefferson said. "I was just thinking, seeing as you have that Fortress of Solitude deal going on at the Fort..."

"I see what you mean," Jody answered. "Sure, if you want. If you don't mind being displayed alongside my...many...athletic trophies..."

"Not at all."

"...plus the statues of my enemies. Staring at 'em really psyches me up in the morning in case I gotta fight 'em later in the day. There are plenty of those there. I'll have to make one of Remus now, now that he's become one of them. But *you're not* one of *them*. Not anymore, anyway. I don't have as many allies as I do enemies in this game, surprisingly, but I keep statues of *them* around, too. I even have one of Sam in case, for some reason, I can't get the real thing. I'd put your statue in *that* room."

"I should *hope* you *would*!"

"But I'm not sure if we can solve the one problem with me trying to make a statue of you."

"What's that?"

"*Where* am I gonna find a mannequin with big enough *boobs* to put your suit on?"

They embraced again, with the same raucous feminine laughter as before, happy again in the comfort of a same shared joke, which they both sincerely hoped would become a more common occurrence in future years.

Sam, who had simply been standing there, feeling somewhat left out, chose this moment to voice his own feelings about his gift.

"Am *I* supposed to put my suit up on display, too?" he asked.

"No!" Jefferson replied. "Yours I want you to *wear*."

"For whose benefit?"

"*Yours*, of course. And Hamilton's."

"Why mine *and* Hamilton's?"

"You two are basically a *couple* now, right?"

"Uh..."

"You're *dating, aren't* you?"

"I...*think* so..."

"Well, the next time you go on a date with Hammy, do your top pelt fur up like mine, and put that suit on. " She laughed raucously, making her later words more obscured. "It'll be like she'll be dating *me*! That little girl will be so surprised, she'll have a *heart attack*!"

"Oh, *really*! Not if *I* do it *first*!"

Hamilton chose this moment to enter the apartment, dressed in a Jefferson suit and wig that made her look exactly like a miniature Jefferson. Taking a stunned Sam by the paw, she lead him out of the apartment, presumably up to hers, leaving an equally stunned Jefferson and Jody alone in the room.

"I'm glad she's on *our* side," Jody observed.

"You ain't whistling Dixie, kid!" added Jefferson.

Fade out for real this time.

About the Author

David Perlmutter is a freelance writer based in Winnipeg, Manitoba, Canada. He is the author of two books on animation history: America 'Toons In: A History of Television Animation (McFarland and Co.) and The Encyclopedia Of American Animated Television Shows (Rowman and Littlefield), as well as essays and works of speculative fiction. .